"Marius, why have you come back like this?"

His mouth curled in the smile she'd always hated. The smile that mocked without amusement. That did not reach the wariness of his eyes.

He said softly, "Because I received an invitation. An offer I couldn't refuse."

"But what do you want?" Lydie's voice almost cracked in desperation.

"Ah." Marius was silent for a moment. "That, I think, remains to be seen." His gaze met hers in a challenge, like a blow. "Maybe I've come back for you."

SARA CRAVEN was born in South Devon, England, and grew up surrounded by books, in a house by the sea. After leaving grammar school, she worked as a local journalist, covering everything from flower shows to murders. She started writing for Harlequin Mills & Boon in 1975. Apart from writing, her passions include films, music, cooking and eating in good restaurants. She now lives in Somerset.

What others have said about Sara Craven:

TOWER OF SHADOWS:
"Ms. Craven does a magnificent job with this daring story of an obsessive love that destroys all it touches...."

—*Romantic Times*

THUNDER ON THE REEF:
"Sara Craven plays a powerful game of cat and mouse with readers in this fascinating web of deception, mystery and passion...."

—*Romantic Times*

DARK APOLLO:
"Sara Craven's latest effort sizzles with sensual tension and dialogue."

—*Romantic Times*

SARA CRAVEN

Deceived

Harlequin Books

TORONTO • NEW YORK • LONDON
AMSTERDAM • PARIS • SYDNEY • HAMBURG
STOCKHOLM • ATHENS • TOKYO • MILAN
MADRID • WARSAW • BUDAPEST • AUCKLAND

ISBN 0-373-11901-1

DECEIVED

First North American Publication 1997.

CHAPTER ONE

LYDIE went up the stairs to the gallery two at a time, the plastic dress carrier bumping against her legs as she ran.

As she pushed open the door, Nell, her partner, turned with an interrogative smile from the ceramics display she was dusting. 'Well?'

Lydie flourished the pastel-striped carrier. 'Mission accomplished.'

'And at the eleventh hour by the sound of it.' Nell paused. 'Your mother's telephoned three times in the past hour, each call more agitated than the last.'

'Austin's birthday party always affects her like this.' Lydie wrinkled her nose. 'I expect the caterers have brought the wrong-shaped canapés.'

'Actually, it sounded rather more serious than that,' said Nell. 'She was in such a state, she actually forgot to snub me. Maybe you'd better ring her.'

Lydie shook her head. 'The crisis can wait till I get home, by which time it will probably be over,' she said drily. 'Sometimes Mama finds the role of Mrs Austin Benedict rather cramping, so when the chance of injecting some extra drama comes along she plays it for all she's worth.'

'Well, you know her better than I do,' Nell said lightly. She nodded at the carrier. 'Going to show me your costume for tonight's mammoth production?'

Lydie hesitated. 'I've got an even better idea. Change your mind and come to the party as my guest,' she urged.

Nell shook her head. 'Can't be done, love.'

'But how the hell are you and Jon going to make up your quarrel if you don't see each other?' Lydie demanded on a note of exasperation.

'We haven't quarrelled,' Nell said patiently. 'We've just put our engagement on hold while Jon decides what to do with his life.'

'In other words, he's to give up his job at Benco Mill.' Lydie's face sobered. 'I don't know if that's possible, Nell.'

'I think it has to be,' Nell said gently. She was a tall girl with a serene face and brown hair gathered into a thick plait. 'He's an artist, Lydie. He doesn't belong at Benco and you know it.'

Lydie bit her lip. 'Yes,' she said. 'I know it. But you don't realise the pressure he's under...'

'Oh, but I do,' Nell said quietly. 'None better. But Jon's got to decide whether to fight it or let himself be dragged into some dead-end future where he'll never be happy or fulfilled.' Her smile was small and wintry. 'And if he settles for that he's not the man for me.'

There was an unhappy silence.

In the eighteen months since they'd started the gallery together Lydie had realised more and more the quiet strength of will which existed behind Nell's laid-back manner. She'd been delighted when she and Jon had begun seeing each other. Jon had dated a lot of girls in his time, none of them seriously. Now, for the first time, Lydie had seen her brother's fickle attention focused and concentrated, watched him mature and grow as never before under Nell's calm tutelage.

Not that it had been roses all the way, she admitted wryly. Nell was gifted and hard-working, and between the pair of them the gallery was managing to pay its way, but her friend had neither the money nor the social background to make her a suitable wife for Debra

Benedict's son. As her mother had made clear from their first meeting.

'That dreadful girl, wandering around like some kind of hippy,' had been her icy verdict. 'If you had to start a business at all, Lydie, couldn't you have found someone at least presentable as your partner?'

'Nell asked me to go into the gallery with her, not the other way round,' Lydie had reminded her levelly.

'It's all the fault of that art college,' Mrs Benedict had gone on fretfully. 'I knew it was a mistake to let you go there.'

It was probably true, Lydie acknowledged ruefully. Jon should have been the one to receive the formal art training, and she should have taken the degree in business studies to which he'd been harnessed. Except that there would have been no job for her at the mill at the end of it. And, at the time, she'd snatched at art training as she would have at anything that took her away from Greystones Park and its memories.

Her stepfather, Austin Benedict, was an old-fashioned man, patriarchal and autocratic where his business was concerned. No matter what legislation might have been passed in the last twenty years, no woman had ever held an executive position at Benco. And Lydie, it had been made clear, was certainly not going to be the first.

The gallery he saw as an indulgence, something to amuse her until she married. It hadn't been easy to convince him that for Nell and herself it was an investment—something they were determined to make into a commercial success.

'I need to justify my existence,' she'd tried to explain.

'You're my stepdaughter.' He'd glared at her from under his heavy brows. 'Round here, that's justification enough.'

Lydie's mother, Debra Hatton, had reached a cross-roads in her acting career when she'd met Austin Benedict. She'd never been in the top flight, in spite of her sultry beauty and distinctive husky voice. She'd been offered only minor film roles, and her theatre career had been on the lightweight side too. She'd had more success with television, landing a role as a neurotic vamp in an early-evening soap, but the meaty parts she'd coveted were being offered more and more to younger women.

She'd been touring in a successful West End comedy when she'd been invited to open a fête in aid of the church restoration fund at Austin Benedict's home, Greystones Park.

She'd accepted reluctantly for the sake of the fee—a woman with two teenage children couldn't afford to be too choosy—but it had turned out to be the wisest decision of her life.

Austin, a childless widower for some years, had never shown the slightest disposition to marry again. But Debra Hatton's wide eyes and slightly ravaged looks had produced a devastating effect on him.

And Debra, looking round at the middle-class solidity of Greystones Park, had seen an end to the struggle and the constant pretence, a finish to the humiliation of having to move out of the limelight and settle for supporting roles, playing women of her own age, or even older. Because to Austin, she'd realised, she would always be the leading lady.

But she didn't brook rivals lightly, Lydie thought ruefully, especially where her beloved Jon was concerned. He was the apple of her eye, the centre of her universe, and probably not even a wealthy heiress would have fulfilled her expectations where he was concerned.

And Nell, in her handmade silver jewellery and Indian cotton skirts, didn't even reach first base.

Now Lydie said soberly, 'Nell—he's terribly miserable without you.'

Nell shook her head again. 'No, his basic unhappiness goes far deeper than that,' she said. 'His whole life is out of kilter. He's a square peg in a round hole, trying all the time to be something he's not—live up to standards he wasn't responsible for setting. And he knows he's the heir apparent too,' she added grimly. 'And it's crucifying him.'

She sighed. 'Oh, why hasn't your stepfather got some convenient male relative to take over from him?'

Lydie looked at the floor. 'He did have once,' she said slowly. 'A nephew.'

Nell stared at her. 'A nephew?' she repeated, her voice sharp with disbelief. 'I've never heard him mentioned before.'

'Nor will you. At least, not at Greystones.' Lydie found that she was sinking her teeth into her lower lip. She released the painful pressure and tried to speak lightly. 'He's the skeleton in the family cupboard, the black sheep of the family. He—left nearly five years ago and hasn't been heard of since.'

'You mean he walked out?'

'Not exactly. There was the most terrible row, and Austin, who'd brought him up ever since his parents died, ordered him out of the house—told him never to darken his door again—the whole bit.'

'What was the row about?'

'The usual sordid mess.' She could still taste blood from her savaged lip. 'He'd got one of the mill girls pregnant, apparently. I—I was still away at school when it all happened. And the subject was forbidden ground ever after.'

'And you just accepted that?' Nell's gaze was searching. 'I don't believe it. You couldn't.'

'I didn't really have a choice,' Lydie defended herself. 'Austin had his first heart attack immediately afterwards, and all the blame for that was put on his quarrel with—with Marius.'

I said his name, she thought, and waited for the pain to strike as it always had when she so much as thought about him. As it still did, she recognised in anguish, her fingers tightening round the handle of the carrier until the knuckles turned white. Five years on, and the wound was still deep—unhealed.

'You'll never mention him again—do you hear?' She could still hear her mother's voice, angry, almost strident. 'Those are Austin's orders and they'll be obeyed. And think yourself lucky, you little fool, that you're not in the same boat as his other teenage tart.'

'So, he just vanished—never to be heard of again?' Nell's voice brought her, wincing, back to the present. 'I find that totally incredible—and rather disturbing.'

'It works both ways, of course,' Lydie said tonelessly. 'Marius has never tried to get in touch either—with any of us. He must have accepted that what he did was unforgivable, at least in Austin's eyes.'

'Or maybe he was just glad to get out from under the Benedict thumb,' Nell retorted, her soft voice grim. 'I wish Jon felt the same.'

She paused. 'Who was the girl?'

'Her name was never actually mentioned,' Lydie acknowledged with difficulty.

'But weren't you curious?'

'Yes—naturally.' And devastated, betrayed, heartbroken. 'But she disappeared at the same time, presumably with Marius. No one was allowed to ask any questions.'

But you didn't want to ask, a sly voice in her head reminded her. Because the questions were hurtful enough in themselves. The answers might have destroyed you.

'Well, it seems extraordinary to me.' Nell gave a quick sigh, then pointed to the bag. 'Now let me have a look at the creation. Rub my nose in what I'll be missing tonight. We may as well close early,' she added. 'It doesn't look as if we're going to be overwhelmed by a last-minute rush.'

There was a mirror in Nell's studio at the rear of the gallery. Lydie gently withdrew the dress from its layers of tissue paper, letting the folds of cream silk slide through her fingers.

Her hands were trembling a little. She'd broken the unwritten law by speaking Marius's name and opened up a real can of worms. Nell's innate sense of justice had been outraged, and in so many ways she was quite right.

Yet at the time, for Austin's sake, there'd seemed no choice but to tacitly accept the curtain of silence which had been drawn over the whole affair. He'd had bypass surgery after that first massive attack and, they'd been warned, he had to be kept free from stress.

They owed him too much to take unnecessary risks. That was indisputable.

She even owed him this dress, she thought wryly as she shook it out.

Yet, in spite of Debra Benedict's pleas to him to slow down, he still went to the mill every day. Nor did he appear to agree with his wife's view that he should shift more executive responsibility onto Jon's shoulders.

'I've set the lad on, and promoted him over better men, my dear,' he'd told her. 'You'll have to settle for that for the time being.'

Debra had seized on his closing words, conveniently ignoring what had gone before, convincing herself that the Benco world was just waiting to be Jon's oyster. She hadn't been able to persuade Austin to adopt both children in the early days of her marriage, but that was no reason why her husband shouldn't leave his company and the estate to his stepson. Especially now that there was no one else.

It was an obsession with her, Lydie thought wearily, holding the dress against herself and turning to study her reflection in the mirror.

Forget the past, she told herself. Think about the dress and the party—and about Hugh, who's probably going to ask you to marry him. Concentrate on that—and the pain will go away. It always has done—eventually. It must now.

Her eyes felt bruised. The cream silk, with its deep square neckline and filmy bell sleeves, looked incongruous against her workaday blue shirt and jeans.

It was almost like a wedding dress, except for the barbaric splash of embroidery across the front of the full skirt—the band of stylised flowers and trailing leaves in gold thread adding a voluptuous element to the purity of the plain silk. A hint, even, of danger.

The neckline was several centimetres short of bridal demureness too, Lydie thought critically. She wouldn't be able to wear a bra. But what Austin didn't know wouldn't grieve him.

All cream and gold, she thought. 'Like a madonna lily.'

The words flicked out of the past like the bite of a whip, flaying her senses, making the breath catch in her throat.

Don't look back, she thought feverishly. Don't let yourself remember. It isn't safe. Not now—not ever...

She held the skirt out slightly, watching the effect with detachment.

Hugh, of course, would love it.

She conjured up his image in her mind with determination. Tall and even fairer than she was, with an easy smile, Hugh Wingate had been in the army, serving in the Falklands and latterly in the Gulf War. On his father's death he'd resigned his commission and come home to look after the family estates. Debra had decided at once that the seventeenth-century Wingate Hall would make a perfect background for Lydie and had spent the previous year trying to bring it about.

Jon, Lydie thought drily, was not the only victim of their mother's manipulative tactics.

But although Hugh had been more than co-operative Lydie had maintained a certain reserve, even though she enjoyed his company and shared a lot of his interests. Many successful marriages, she knew, had been based on far less.

But she wasn't in love with Hugh and she knew it. His kisses, while agreeable, left her only faintly stirred, and she'd had not the slightest difficulty in resisting his urging her to carry their relationship to a more intimate level. If and when they became officially engaged, the pressure, she supposed, would increase, and she would have to surrender herself.

But maybe that was what she needed, she thought broodingly. Perhaps the only way to erase the past, and the pain, was to commit herself to another relationship. To begin her life as a woman all over again.

She stared at herself. It could be that she was never to know again the same wild intensity of feeling she'd experienced five years ago; that what she felt for Hugh was as good as it was going to get. Well, so be it. Hugh would never feel short-changed anyway, she vowed inwardly. She would make sure of that.

Security, she thought—that's what matters above all. She could remember only too clearly the various cheap flats, the uncertainty of school holidays, the terrifying fluctuation of finances which had marked their childhood, could understand why Debra, her career in decline, her spectacular looks beginning to fade, had grabbed with both hands at the florid Edwardian comfort of Greystones and Austin's unstinting devotion.

If Hugh proposed tonight as her mother was sure he intended, then she'd accept. Turn Austin's birthday into a double celebration.

She turned away from the mirror and waltzed out into the gallery, the dress held against her.

'I'll have my hair up tonight,' she announced. 'But you'll have to imagine the rest of it.'

She checked, her hand flying to her mouth in sudden embarrassment. She hadn't heard him arrive but there was a last-minute customer just the same.

There was a man's tall figure standing beside Nell near the cash desk.

God, she thought with vexation, snatching the dress away as if it were stinging her and throwing it over her arm. What an idiot I must look.

Flushing deeply, she said, 'I'm sorry. I didn't realise anyone else was here.'

'Don't apologise.' The deep voice was husky with amusement. 'I wouldn't have missed the performance for the world.'

Poised for retreat, Lydie felt instead as if she'd suddenly been turned to stone. She felt her lips parting in a silent gasp, her green eyes widening endlessly as he moved without haste towards her.

The overhead light shining directly on him showed thick, faintly curling dark hair and a lean, tanned face, against which his grey eyes were as cold and hard as a winter sky.

'Cream and gold,' Marius Benedict said softly. 'Just like a madonna lily.' And he smiled at her.

All the breath seemed to catch in her throat. Then she moved, swiftly, clumsily, her hand swinging up in front of her as if to ward him off. And a bowl with a vivid blue glaze went smashing to the floor.

'Oh, no,' Lydie wailed, and knelt to pick up the pieces.

'Careful you don't cut your hand.' Nell rushed over to her. 'And keep your dress off the floor. It'll mark.'

'I'm afraid I startled her,' the deep voice said. 'You must let me pay for the damage.'

'These things happen.' Nell was philosophical. She gave Lydie a swift hug. 'You pop off home. I'll clear up.'

'All right,' Lydie managed. She got stiffly to her feet, not convinced that her legs would support her.

'Let me help.' He walked forward, his hand reaching for her arm.

Lydie recoiled. 'I can manage.' Her voice sounded breathless—like a stranger's.

He halted, his brows lifting. 'Then can I at least offer you a lift?'

She swallowed. 'Thank you, but I have my own car.'

'Of course you have,' he said softly. 'How stupid of me. Then I'll just—see you later.'

She could feel his eyes following her as she walked the endless distance back to the studio. She dragged the heavy curtain over the doorway with a rattle of protesting rings, wishing with all her heart that it were a door she could close—and lock. Then she stood, motionless, among the familiar scents of oil paints and turpentine, feeling like an alien in some strange and dangerous country. Her mouth was bone-dry, her heart pounding like a sledgehammer.

Marius, she thought. *Marius* back in Thornshaugh after five years of silence. It couldn't be happening.

Only a few minutes ago she'd broken the taboo and said his name. And now here he was, as if she'd conjured him like a spirit from some vast and echoing limbo.

Speak of the devil, they said, and he's bound to appear.

With feverish hands she bundled the dress back into its tissue wrapping. 'Madonna lily'. The words throbbed in her head. She could never wear it now. Never even wanted to see it again.

There'd be something else in her wardrobe—the little black number she'd bought to have dinner with Hugh last week. She could dress that up, somehow. Her mind ran in feverish circles, trying to focus on trivialities and shut out the clamour in her brain.

What—*what* in the name of God could Marius be doing back here? Thornshaugh was barred to him, so what could he possibly hope to gain by simply—turning up like this?

Unless, of course, it wasn't that simple at all.

Suddenly, it hurt to breathe.

'See you later,' he'd said. Not 'see you around'. That could have real significance.

She glimpsed herself in the mirror again, and paused. She looked like death. Her face was white and her eyes twice their normal size.

What had he seen? she wondered suddenly. How had she changed? She'd shed every last trace of never very evident puppy fat a long time ago, and her fair hair had been skilfully highlighted, but apart from that there wasn't much to separate her from the naïve, trusting seventeen-year-old he'd betrayed and left behind.

He looked older than his thirty years, she thought, striving for objectivity. The lines beside his mouth seemed to be slashed deeper, but not, she decided, with laughter. His hair was overlong for Thornshaugh tastes. But then, that had always been a bone of contention with Austin...

She cut the memories right there, grabbing up her shoulder bag and turning to the door. Then the curtain was thrust back and Nell came in.

'It's all right, he's gone,' she said drily. 'So that's the prodigal nephew.'

Lydie ran her tongue over her dry lips. 'What the hell's he doing here?'

'Buying that expensive stoneware plate we thought we'd never sell—apparently for a birthday present.' Nell let that sink in. 'You obviously weren't expecting to see him.'

Lydie said hoarsely, 'Never in this world.'

Nell grinned. 'Your stepfather's birthday seems to be turning into a surprise party.'

'It can't be true,' Lydie said, half to herself. 'There's been no sign—no word for five whole years. Austin can't be expecting him—surely he'd have said something to prepare us—warn us...?'

'You'd think so,' Nell agreed. 'But communication doesn't seem to be a Benedict strong point. Maybe Austin's just ordered a fatted calf as the centrepiece of the buffet, leaving people to draw their own conclusions.' She examined a fleck on one of her nails. 'So—what will your mother have to say—and Jon?'

Lydie swallowed. 'I—don't know. At least—Jon won't mind. He and Marius got on, I think. And Jon was at university when the big row blew up. He—we were both stunned when we found out Marius had—just—gone like that,' she added with difficulty.

'At the very least,' Nell commented caustically.

Lydie looked at the floor. 'You can't imagine what it was like,' she said huskily. 'Austin was in Intensive Care and Mother was having one fit of hysterics after another and blaming Marius for everything.'

And he did vanish, she thought, without a trace. Without one word of goodbye. With no excuse or explanation from that day to this.

'So you just went with the flow.' Nell was silent for a moment. 'Well, he's certainly prospered in his absence. As well as the plate, he insisted on paying for that bowl you broke—in cash. He was wearing a platinum watch too,' she added, as if that settled the matter.

Lydie forced a wan smile. 'Good.'

Nell gave her a questioning look, then shrugged. 'Well, you'd better run along and join the celebrations—if that's really the word I'm looking for.'

Maybe, Lydie thought grimly, I'll just keep running.

She had a parking space in the yard behind the gallery building. She tossed the dress carrier into the rear of her Corsa, then slid into the driving seat. She crossed her arms limply on the steering wheel and bent forward, hiding her face against them.

For almost five long years she'd tried to forget—to put the whole agonising memory out of her mind. Now, it seemed, she had no choice but to remember—Marius.

CHAPTER TWO

'MADONNA lily'.

The words echoed inside her skull like the beat of a hammer.

She had, of course, never expected to see him again.

At first she'd waited, hoping, praying, in spite of what he'd done, for some contact—some message. But the weeks had stretched into months and there had been only silence.

Marius had gone, leaving her behind, and nothing that had happened between them, nothing that had been said or done, had made the slightest difference to his decision.

That was what she'd slowly learned to live with during five endless years—that he hadn't even cared enough to be faithful.

What a fool, she thought rawly. What a blind, trusting idiot.

She'd been eleven when they'd first met, a gawky, bewildered child trying to come to terms with the sudden overwhelming change in her circumstances.

One day she'd been an unhappy boarder in a second-rate school outside London, the next she'd been whisked up to the north of England in a Rolls-Royce driven by a gruff, grey-haired man who wore expensive suits and smoked cigars, and whom her mother had introduced as 'Your new stepfather, darling. Austin—' she'd turned to him, smiling brilliantly '—do you want Lydie to call you Daddy or Uncle?'

19

'Neither.' The fierce eyes had softened as they'd looked at the small, wan face. 'You can call me Austin, lass. Most other people do.'

Greystones Park, seen for the first time under heavy skies and driving rain, had seemed oppressive—even threatening.

Jon wasn't there—he was staying at his current school until he'd finished the examinations he was taking—and she felt totally isolated and friendless. Her mother and stepfather were too wrapped up in each other to spare her much attention, and she was left very much to the mercies of Mrs Arnthwaite, the housekeeper, who had not taken kindly to having a new mistress of the house foisted on her.

Mrs Arnthwaite knew better than to let her discontent show to her employer, and his new wife, but she let Lydie bear the brunt of it in numerous little unkindnesses.

Lydie was told curtly to 'get out of the road' so many times that she began to feel as if there wasn't a corner in any of the numerous rooms where she could take refuge even for a moment.

So much so that, coming along the landing one day, she heard the housekeeper approaching and promptly shot through the nearest door, straight under the bed which stood conveniently handy.

Hidden by the valance in the dusty dark, she waited silently until, overwhelmed by loneliness, she cried herself to sleep.

When she woke up there was a light in the room and someone was moving around. She tried to keep still, because if it was Mrs Arnthwaite she'd be in more trouble. But the dust under the bed was tickling her nose, and eventually she gave vent to an uncontrollable sneeze.

Someone lifted the valance. A male voice said, 'What the hell...?' and Lydie was hauled out unceremoniously.

She sat on the carpet and looked up at him. He was very tall, was her first thought, with legs that seemed to go on for ever. She was used to good-looking men, but the dark face looking down at her was more striking than conventionally handsome. The lines of his mouth, cheekbones and jaw were sharply delineated and his nose was like a beak. More a tough guy, she thought, categorising him in the only way she knew, than a romantic lead.

She knew who it must be. Austin had spoken a lot about his nephew, Marius, who was away at Oxford working for his finals, but who'd be home on his first free weekend to meet his new aunt, and she could count on it.

And this, of course, was his room. Lydie had been told so when they had been shown round the first day. She'd also got the impression that it was some kind of holy ground. And now she'd been discovered trespassing there. She couldn't begin to imagine what would happen to her.

But when she dared to look at him he didn't seem all that angry. In fact, he seemed to be having trouble keeping his face straight.

'What were you doing under there?' he asked.

'There was nowhere else to go,' she said. 'I—I fell asleep. I'm sorry.'

'You will be when you get downstairs,' he said drily. 'You missed your tea and got put on report. Austin's starting to talk about dragging the river for you.'

'Are they very cross?' she asked with apprehension.

'More worried than angry. Come on; I'll go down with you and you can make your peace.' He helped her up, his eyes narrowing as he studied the grimy streaks of woe visible on her face. 'We'd better clean you up first.' He opened the door to his private bathroom and pushed her gently inside, standing over her while she washed her face and hands.

'Here.' He tossed her a towel. It smelled faintly of cologne—the same harsh, rather musky scent she'd noticed as he'd picked her up from the floor. It suited him far better than some of the more florid scents her mother's leading men used, she thought, burying her face in the towel, breathing in luxuriously.

'Thank you,' she said politely as she handed it back. She looked up at him, letting her eyes widen and the corner of her mouth curve upwards slightly as she'd seen Debra do so many times. And saw his brows snap together.

'You're far too young for tricks like that.' He tapped the tip of her nose with a finger, his mouth twisting. 'One charmer in the family is quite enough to be going on with.'

It sounded almost like a joke, but she sensed that it wasn't really meant to be funny. She found herself wondering with an intuition beyond her years whether Marius Benedict really welcomed his uncle's marriage and the unlooked-for expansion of the family group.

Downstairs, Marius shrugged off the inevitable recriminations over her disappearance, saying easily that she'd made herself a secret den and fallen asleep in it.

'A den?' Debra repeated, as if the word needed translation. 'But where?'

Watching him, Lydie saw that his cool smile didn't reach his eyes. He said quite gently, 'If I told you that, it wouldn't be a secret any longer.' Then he looked at Lydie and his smile warmed into a reassuring grin.

From that moment she'd been his slave.

Looking back over the years, Lydie could see wryly what a nuisance the unstinting adoration of a small girl must have been to him. But if he'd been irritated he'd never let it show, treating her generally with an amused if slightly distant kindness.

As she'd grown older, and more perceptive, she'd become aware of his reserve—that almost tangible barrier that divided him from the rest of the world. She'd wondered sometimes if his being an orphan had created it. After losing both parents he'd had no softening female influence in his life, unless you counted Mrs Arnthwaite, which Lydie privately thought was impossible.

And Debra's invasion had made things worse, not better. Lydie had realised that quite early on. Sensed the underlying tensions, and her mother's simmering, barely concealed resentment of the young man who'd been her husband's main priority for so many years.

She came first with him now; that went without saying. Austin's pride in her was enormous, and he indulged her to the hilt.

But that hadn't been enough for Debra.

Because it should have been Jon next in line—Jon, the golden, the beautiful, the favoured child. Lydie hadn't needed to be told this. She'd always existed in her brother's shadow, but she loved him enough not to mind, admiring the good looks and talent he himself took so much for granted.

And yet Marius had been Austin's heir, who would fill his shoes at Greystones and eventually take over the running of the mill. No alternative had been even considered—at least, not then.

It had not been all plain sailing between Austin and Marius either. Austin had taken the mill which his great-grandfather had founded and built it into an amazing success. The Benco Mill was Thornshaugh's biggest employer, and the steadiest.

Marius, however, had wanted to move away from the autocratic, paternalistic style of management to greater worker participation. He'd fought too for the latest machinery and office systems to be installed. He'd introduced a private health scheme and ordered a complete overhaul of the firm's social club, ensuring that it was a comfortable venue for the whole family.

There had invariably been furious arguments but they'd always been resolved. In spite of his protests that 'what was good enough for my father should be good enough for anyone' Austin had recognised that no business could stand still and had given ground, albeit grudgingly.

He'd even begun to talk of retirement...

And then, not long after Austin's sixtieth birthday party, there'd been that final, terminal, furiously bitter quarrel, and Marius had gone, as if into thin air, his room stripped of his clothes and belongings, his destination a mystery. It hadn't even been known if he'd travelled alone.

And Austin, his normally ruddy complexion suddenly grey, had made it dogmatically clear that the matter would end there.

It had been a nine days' wonder in Thornshaugh, only superseded by the shock of Austin's sudden collapse. Life had become a chaos of ambulance sirens, doctors' hushed voices and endless telephone calls of enquiry.

In the middle of it all, Lydie had tried to comfort her mother as she'd waited to be admitted to see her husband in Intensive Care.

Debra had turned on her. 'This is his fault.' Her voice had risen, cracking. 'Your precious Marius. This is what he's done. He's a murderer. You dare mention him again...'

Lydie had never dared after that. Austin had been very ill and her worry over him had had to take precedence over her own grinding pain and bewilderment—her crying need to make sense of what had happened.

She drew a quivering sigh, and lifted her head from the steering wheel, gazing ahead of her with unseeing eyes.

'Are y'all right, Miss Hatton?' The security man appeared beside the car, peering curiously at her. 'Only I was going to lock up the yard, like.'

'Yes, Bernie.' Lydie started her engine. 'You do that.' She backed up with extra care because she was shaking inside, and headed home.

Greystones Park was a hive of activity. The gardener was fastening up the last loop of fairy lights in the trees along the drive as Lydie passed, and there were caterers' and florists' vans everywhere.

She put the car away and slipped through the side-door and up to her room.

As she opened the door, Debra Benedict wheeled round from the window. 'Where have you been?' Her voice was accusing. She was wearing a black silk kimono sprinkled with flowers and was puffing nervously at a cigarette. 'Didn't that girl give you my message? Dear God, Lydie, have you the least idea what's happened?'

'Yes.' Lydie paused warily. 'I know. Marius has turned up.'

'You know? You mean he's been in touch with you—you were aware of what was planned?' Debra's voice lifted in furious incredulity.

'Of course not. He came into the gallery just before we closed,' Lydie said flatly. 'I thought I was seeing things.'

Debra's laugh held a hint of hysteria. 'Unfortunately, my dear, he's all too bloody real.'

'Does Austin know yet?'

Debra drew unevenly on her cigarette. 'Know? It's all his doing. He's invited him here—to his birthday party—without a single word to me—to anyone.' This time her laugh was angry. 'Simply told me this afternoon there'd be an extra guest. Just as if my opinion, my feelings didn't count. God knows how long he's been hatching this,' she added venomously.

'But isn't it for the best?' Lydie ventured. 'He's Austin's only relative after all.'

'Don't be a fool.' Debra glared at her. 'You think I'm going to go along with all this absurd "forgive and forget" routine? Start mouthing clichés about blood being thicker than water?' She almost spat the words. 'Let him walk back in here and—cheat Jon out of everything he's worked for—slaving in that damned mill? Like hell I will. Austin must be going senile.'

'That,' Lydie told her levelly, 'is a shameful remark.'

'Don't you dare preach at me.' Debra lit another cigarette from the stub of the last one. 'You don't know what's at stake here.'

'Maybe I do at that.' Lydie went over to the wardrobe and retrieved the black dress and the black court shoes with the spiky heels which went with it. 'Jon may welcome Marius's return. Have you considered that?'

'No.' Debra dismissed the possibility with contempt. 'He knows exactly which side his bread is buttered. If Marius gets a foothold at Benco, Jon's going to end up in some menial position or out of a job altogether.'

And Nell would be delighted, Lydie thought drily as she selected a fragile black teddy together with a suspender belt and stockings from her lingerie drawer and tossed them onto the bed. Although she'd probably prefer Jon to make the decision on his own behalf rather than be squeezed out, she mentally amended.

'And what about me?' Debra went on restively. 'Next thing I know that beastly lawyer will be up here again, droning on about suitable provision and annuities. I'll end my days in some ghastly private hotel on the south coast, watching the price of my shares with all the other widows, having to think twice about everything I spend. Just like the old days.'

Her mouth was trembling, her eyes almost blank.

Selfish she might be, mercenary she certainly was, but all the same Lydie felt a flicker of compassion for her. Mrs Benedict, chatelaine of Greystones Park, was the best part Debra had ever been offered, and she'd played it magnificently to a small but devoted audience.

But if anything happened to Austin the curtain would come down for her mother too. Unless Jon, not Marius, was confirmed as Austin's heir...

She tried to make her tone light. 'Don't write Austin off so soon. He's a tough old stick. He'll probably outlive the lot of us.'

She paused. 'And you don't know yet—none of us do—exactly what this reconciliation means. It's been five years, after all. Marius has another life now—maybe—other commitments.' The words made her throat ache. A child, certainly, she thought. Maybe a wife too.

Aloud she went on, 'He may not want to come back to Thornshaugh on a permanent basis.'

'Don't be a fool.' Debra tossed her cigarette through the open window into the dusk-shaded shrubbery below. 'Of course he does. Wouldn't you?'

Lydie shook her head. 'I've no idea what Marius thinks—or wants.' Although I thought I knew once, God help me, she added silently.

Her mother's mouth tightened to a slit. 'Austin's made him cancel his hotel reservation and move back here. Actually into his old room, if you please.' She drove her clenched fist into the palm of her other hand. 'I just cannot believe this is really happening. It's like a nightmare. Austin was always so adamant—so totally determined. I thought we were rid of Marius for good.'

Lydie winced inwardly. 'He hasn't given you a reason—any kind of explanation?'

'His exact words were, "I've made a decision."' Debra's laugh was metallic. 'And Austin's decisions, however arbitrary, are to be accepted without question.'

The only person who'd ever argued with him was Marius himself, Lydie thought.

She glanced at her watch. 'I don't think the situation will be helped by our being late for dinner,' she said quietly. 'I'm going to run my bath.'

'My God, you're cool,' Debra said acidly. 'Don't you think it won't affect you if Marius moves back and takes over. We're all going to feel the draught, my lady.'

And with that she was gone.

Oh, it would affect her, Lydie thought drily a few minutes later as she tried to relax in the warm water, but certainly not in the way her mother thought.

Although there could be a problem over the gallery.

Thornshaugh, with its steep, cobbled streets and well-preserved buildings left over from the Industrial Revolution, was attractive enough to form part of the itinerary of tourists drawn to Yorkshire's West Riding by the Brontë Parsonage at Haworth or the Curry Trail at Bradford.

The gallery was situated on the first floor of a former Benco warehouse, sharing the premises with a popular boutique at ground level, a home bakery and various workshops occupied by woodcarvers, candlemakers and hand weavers.

They sold mainly paintings, prints and pottery by local artists and craftsmen, including Nell herself. And, although Lydie and Nell had refused to sell souvenirs, they'd made sure they stocked the kind of small, unusual but inexpensive items which tourists would want as mementoes or gifts, and these went like hot cakes.

When the bank had looked down its nose and talked about the recession, Lydie had turned instead to her stepfather for the initial loan to finance the enterprise. And, to Debra's thinly veiled chagrin, he'd agreed to put up the money.

The gallery was managing to keep its head above water mainly because Lydie didn't draw a full salary yet. Not that she needed to, because she lived at Greystones and Austin insisted on making her an allowance, firmly steamrollering over her objections.

Another of his decisions, Lydie thought ruefully. But she compromised by spending as frugally as possible, although the dress still abandoned in its carrier in the back of her car had been an exception to that self-imposed rule. And perhaps she'd be able to return it anyway.

Now she found herself wishing that she'd stuck to her guns, managed on whatever pittance she could have drawn from the company.

She dried herself and put on her underwear, drawing the stockings slowly over her smooth legs, remembering another time five years ago when she'd dressed for Austin's birthday party with her heart performing strange, shaky somersaults inside.

She'd been allowed home from school specially, and had spent every penny she'd saved on a new dress that time too.

The one she'd wanted then had also been black—with spangles, she thought; sleek as a second skin. Black was the colour of sophistication; she'd wanted to show

Marius that she wasn't a child any longer but a woman, ready—eager for love.

Her hand faltered slightly with the blusher she was applying.

But the boutique owner had tactfully steered her away from that and into a much simpler model in jade-green, almost the same colour as her eyes.

Now she paid minute attention to them with shadow and liner, accentuating their shape and lustre, according the same attention to detail to the colour she painted onto her mouth. Tonight the mask had to be perfect. Impenetrable.

Five years ago, her face had been highlighted by an inner brilliance, with little need for cosmetics. The tiny bodice with its shoestring straps had flattered the sweet flare of her breasts, and the short, full skirt had swirled enticingly. She'd held it out in both hands and turned slowly in front of the mirror, imagining herself dancing in Marius's arms. Seeing the smile in his eyes when she told him she loved him. Hearing the tenderness in his voice when he told her he felt the same...

Lydie stood up abruptly, reaching for the black dress, and zipped herself into it, smoothing it over her hips. Black, she thought; the colour of mourning. For the death of faith and innocence. The ending of a girl's dream.

She took a long look at herself. Her hair was drawn up into a sleek topknot, with only a few random tendrils softening the line around the nape of her neck and her ears. She had disguised the real shadows around her eyes and painted on a smile. Who could ask for anything more? she wondered with irony.

She opened the door and stepped into the passage just as Marius emerged from his own room a few yards away.

Lydie kept a hand behind her, holding the handle of her bedroom door, feeling the hard metal bite into her flesh, letting one pain combat another as she absorbed the bitter familiarity of him in a dinner jacket and black tie. Formal evening clothes had always suited him, accentuating the width of his shoulders and the leanness of his hips.

That other night, long ago, she'd watched, breathless with a new, secret excitement, as he'd walked towards her, wanting only to run to him, to feel his arms closing around her.

Now her mouth was dry and she felt deadly cold as she recognised the distance that hurt and betrayal had imposed between them.

'Good evening, Madonna Lily.' His brows lifted as his glance examined her. 'Or should I call you Black Orchid tonight?'

'Neither.'

'No?' He affected a sigh. 'Yet there was a time...'

'A time long past.' She managed to control the faint tremor in her voice.

'How strange,' he said slowly, 'that you should think so, when to me it feels like yesterday.'

Lydie lifted her chin. She said rawly, 'Marius—for God's sake—what are you doing here? Why have you come back like this?'

His mouth curled in the smile she'd always hated. The smile that mocked without amusement. That did not reach the wariness in his eyes.

He said softly, 'Because I received an invitation. An offer I couldn't refuse.'

'But what do you want?' Her voice almost cracked in desperation.

'Ah.' Marius was silent for a moment. 'That, I think, remains to be seen, Madonna Lily.' His gaze met hers in a challenge like a blow. 'Maybe I've come back for you.'

Her head went back with shock, and she felt her mouth frame the word no. Then she turned and headed blindly for the stairs, the jeer of his laughter following her like a shadow.

CHAPTER THREE

LYDIE didn't wait to see if Marius was following. She headed straight for the drawing room, hesitating momentarily at the door while she dragged together the rags of her composure.

Did he really think that he could walk back into this house—back into her life—as if the past five silent years meant nothing? As if he'd never been away?

She'd been young then, and vulnerable. But now she had her future planned, her emotions under control. And Marius had no part in her life. That was the only certainty in a reeling world.

The sooner I'm out of this house, she thought grimly, the better.

She pushed open the door and went into the room.

Jon was there alone, decanter in hand.

'Hi, doll.' His smile was forced. 'Welcome to the family reunion, and you're more than welcome, believe me.' He squinted at the measure of whisky he'd just poured into his glass. 'I wonder what other grisly surprises are in store for us?'

Lydie said with constraint, 'I thought you liked Marius.'

'Like the rest of us, I suspect I never knew him.' He sounded reflective as he poured her usual dry sherry. 'Although that's an omission we'll all have ample opportunity to repair from now on.' He handed her her glass then drank some whisky. 'Our mama is fit to be tied, of course.'

Lydie nodded. 'I've seen her.' She paused. 'I think she's overreacting.'

'Or just overacting.' Jon reached for the decanter again. 'But you can't blame her for being shocked. For once she looked at her hand and failed to find Austin twined round her little finger. That makes him unpredictable, and therefore dangerous.'

Lydie twisted the stem of the crystal glass in her fingers. She said, 'She's always blamed Marius—the quarrel—for Austin's heart attack.'

Jon laughed derisively. 'That's only part of it. She and Marius were at odds from the start, ever since she started treating her marriage like a pools win.' He waved his glass around. 'This house, for starters. She had it completely done over—got rid of all the family stuff that had been here for generations. Marius, apparently, found this clean sweep slightly insensitive.'

'I didn't realise that,' Lydie said slowly. 'I knew there'd been changes, of course.'

'You were too young to see what was going on. Apparently the business was having problems at the time but Mama was oblivious. And she resented the fact that Marius couldn't also be brought to heel with a flutter of her eyelashes. Plus he was tactless enough to let her see he thought she'd exceeded her sell-by date.'

Lydie bit her lip. 'Yes, I understood that at least.'

'So, when Austin finally cancelled the blank cheque and made her an allowance instead, she blamed Marius.' Jon held his glass up to the light, admiring the rich amber of the whisky. 'Although I'd guess it was pressure from the accountants and the bank. However besotted Austin was, he wasn't going to let her bankrupt him.'

He shook his head. 'But with Marius banished to outer darkness Mama must have thought the gravy train would eventually be running on the old track again. Hence her distress at his return.'

'But you're not happy about it either.'

'Are you?' He gave her a searching look. 'I recall you had it pretty bad for him at one time.'

Lydie moved an evasive shoulder. 'An adolescent crush.' She didn't look at him. 'Maybe I've come back for you.' The words seemed to hammer in her brain, threatening her. 'Water under the bridge,' she threw defiantly at the sudden shiver whispering down her spine.

'I hope for your sake that's true. I can't imagine that his wilderness years will have softened his attitude towards our side of the family.'

'What about you?'

Jon's lips tightened. 'I've put in five years' hard graft at that bloody mill. I don't want someone else to have my place in the sun while I'm relegated to the sidelines— or worse,' he added grimly.

Lydie put down her untouched glass. 'You don't think this would be a good time to make a complete break?'

He shot her an angry look. 'You've been letting Nell brainwash you, darling. I'm staying where I am and fighting my corner. And you should do the same. Because if anything happens to Austin Marius will have us out of here before the coffin lid's screwed down.'

Lydie found herself wincing at his crudeness. She said, half to herself, 'I wonder where he's been—all this time?'

'Not letting the grass grow under his feet, that's for sure. You should see the car he's driving these days.' He paused. 'As a matter of interest, you didn't persuade Nell to change her mind and come tonight?'

His tone was elaborately casual, and Lydie softened in spite of herself. 'No, but I did try.'

'Never mind,' he said, with a shrug. 'I'll have to rely on Chivas Regal for company instead.'

The door opened and Debra Benedict came in. She was wearing a silver dress and there were amethysts around her throat and in her ears. She checked, looking round her.

'Where are they?' she asked sharply.

'Presumably in the study, having another round of peace talks.' Jon waved the decanter at her. 'Drinkies?'

'No, thank you, and you've had quite enough as well.' Debra gave him a warning frown. 'Don't play into that man's hands by getting drunk tonight, for heaven's sake.' She paused. 'I'll get Mrs Arnthwaite to announce dinner now.'

'Thus killing numerous birds with one stone.' Jon put the decanter down. 'OK, Mama, I surrender.'

But I don't, Lydie thought, lifting her chin. I can't. I'm going to fight—and go on fighting. Because, whatever happens, I can't let him anywhere near me again. I dare not.

Austin Benedict looked relaxed as he took his seat at the head of the table. Marius, seating himself opposite Lydie, appeared merely inscrutable.

'Well, this is pleasant,' Austin remarked, unfolding his napkin. 'The calm before the storm. How many people are coming to this shindig afterwards, Deb?'

Mrs Benedict cleared her throat. 'Over two hundred— if they all turn up.'

'Oh, they'll come.' He nodded. 'Even the ones who never intended to. Word soon gets round this valley, and they'll all be here to see for themselves.' He transferred his attention to Lydie. 'That's a sombre colour for a party, lass. This is a celebration, not a wake, and don't you forget it.'

The warning note was unmistakable. So was the bottle of Krug, cooling on ice on the sideboard. Lydie felt

Marius's ironic gaze seek hers across the table and faint colour rose in her face.

Austin addressed himself to the company at large. 'We present a united front tonight,' he said abruptly. 'What happened five years ago is no one's business but our own. I want that clear.' He swept the table with a fierce gaze. 'No recriminations or prying into what's over. We can't call time back to alter things, so we look to the future. Right?'

'As the future's been mentioned,' Jon said softly, 'may I ask what office I'll be occupying on Monday? When I left today I was sales director, but things seem to be changing so fast suddenly...'

Lydie swore under her breath. That's not the way to handle it, you fool, she castigated him silently.

It was Marius who answered, his tone even. 'You'll have the same job. But I'd like a departmental report for the last six months on my desk by mid-week.'

'Certainly.' Jon sketched a parody of a salute. 'And what desk precisely is that?'

'The managing director's,' said Austin. 'I'm continuing as chairman only from now on. The board's been informed.'

Lydie stole a look at her mother. All the natural colour had faded from her face, leaving two harsh streaks of blusher high on her cheekbones. For a moment Lydie tensed, thinking that Debra was going to explode, then, with a palpable effort, her mother reached out and rang the small handbell for Mrs Arnthwaite to bring in the soup.

It was, Lydie thought, the worst dinner she'd ever sat through. Even the glory of the champagne couldn't lift her spirits. As she pushed the food round her plate, she felt as if she was drowning in undercurrents, suffocated by the silence of her mother and brother.

Marius chatted equably to his uncle on safely neutral topics—Yorkshire's performance in the county cricket championship, enquiries about former friends and acquaintances—but Lydie wasn't fooled.

Across the expanse of crystal, silverware and flowers—Austin's favourite white roses arranged in a bowl—she could feel his awareness of her, like the touch of his hand on her naked skin. She was conscious of his gaze resting on her, as if willing her to lift her eyes and return his scrutiny.

Don't look at him, she adjured herself frantically. Pretend the chair is still empty.

Her heart was hammering violently. She wanted to get to her feet, sweep away the flowers and every other artificial barrier and scream at him, Who was she? Where is she now? If you had her, why did you take me? Was she better in bed than I was? All the teeming questions that had plagued her like a recurring fever, and which she could never ask, of course.

Water under the bridge, she'd told Jon, and it had to be true. They weren't the same people any more. She was no longer a trusting child, driven beyond reason by her first love. She'd grown up fast in a school of anguished and bitter betrayal. She was old enough and wise enough now to recognise danger when she saw it, and take avoiding action.

And, whatever Marius had been before, their previous confrontation warned her that he was a hazard now, not merely to herself but to all of them.

She risked a covert glance at him from under her lashes and found him watching her quite openly, the firm lips twisting in a mixture of mockery and triumph as their eyes met—clashed.

You see? he seemed to be telling her. I won in the end. All I had to do was wait.

And that, Lydie thought furiously, waving away the Peaches Cardinal that Mrs Arnthwaite was offering, was my first mistake tonight. My first—and my last.

Guests began arriving for the party an hour later. An enormous marquee had been erected on the rear lawn, with a floor laid for dancing, and the small band was already tuning up. The buffet had been set out in the conservatory, which also housed one of the bars.

It was the usual gargantuan spread—like an orgy scene from an old Hollywood epic, Lydie thought wryly, viewing the rich dark ribs of beef and the golden-brown turkeys jostling for position next to honey-roast hams and poached salmon glazed in aspic and cucumber. And that was quite apart from the mousses, pâtés, vol-au-vents and vast array of salads.

No one had ever actually fallen in the swimming pool and drowned from overeating but there could always be a first time.

Her mouth ached from smiling, and she dodged and evaded so many questions about Marius's sudden re-appearance that she felt like a heavyweight champion's sparring partner.

Hugh Wingate was among the first to arrive. Guilt sent her hurtling into his arms as she realised she hadn't given him a single thought up to that moment.

'I'd have been here even sooner if I'd known that was going to be my reception,' he told her throatily. He paused. 'I hear Austin's had a surprise present.'

Lydie forced a smile. 'It's tonight's sole topic of conversation—quite naturally, I suppose.'

'Maybe we can give them something else to chatter about.'

He was going to propose to her. For a moment her mind went blank with relief. It was the lifeline she needed. It was safety—sanity in a reeling world.

But was it what she really wanted? asked a small, tormenting voice in her head.

I'll worry about that later, she thought, and turned to greet some more arrivals.

Austin's birthday parties traditionally began with a waltz, preceded by a few words of welcome. This year, thought Lydie, you could have heard a pin drop. She glanced at Jon, her brows snapping together. In spite of their mother's admonitions, he was clearly halfway to being plastered already.

She kicked him discreetly. 'Give it a rest, can't you?'

He shrugged, some of the contents of his glass slopping onto his dinner jacket. 'Why worry? The contest's over, and I came a poor second.'

Lydie bit her lip. 'Well, make sure you don't get stripped of the silver medal too.'

Austin cleared his throat. 'It's wonderful to see so many friends here tonight. I'm past the age when birthdays are something to celebrate, so tonight's party is to welcome my nephew back amongst us all. Apart from my personal pleasure at having him home where he belongs, from next week our customers will have a new managing director to deal with.' He let the rustle of interest and speculation subside, then added, 'Now let's enjoy ourselves.'

Like drawing a line at the bottom of a balance sheet, Lydie thought. And it would be a brave soul who'd dare question the accounts after that.

She watched him step down onto the floor, holding out a hand to his wife. Amid a ripple of applause they opened the dancing. Other couples followed, and Lydie turned to look for Hugh, only to find her way blocked by Marius.

Her throat closed up in sudden panic.

His voice was politely formal. 'May I have the honour?'

Without waiting for her answer he drew her into his arms and onto the floor.

'Austin's orders.' His lips grazed her ear, sending an unwelcome tremor of response quivering through her. 'In the interest of family unity.'

She said frostily, 'Of course.'

'And my own inclination,' he added, a thread of amusement in his voice. He swung her effortlessly round. 'I suppose I could say—just like old times.'

'No,' she said deliberately and distinctly. 'You could not.'

'And they say absence makes the heart grow fonder,' he mocked.

'Then they, whoever they are, should think again,' Lydie said shortly.

Absence tears you apart and leaves you to bleed, she thought. Absence makes you cry into your pillow at night and stumble round like a zombie during the day. Absence destroys.

'I get the impression that, left to you, the red carpet would have remained unrolled,' the softly taunting voice went on.

She hunched a shoulder. 'What do you expect?'

'Very little.' He paused. 'This reconciliation was not actually my idea.'

That jolted her, and she let it show, her eyes lifting to his in sudden startled query.

'No? Then how did Austin manage to find you?'

'I haven't asked him,' Marius drawled. 'I imagine he's been keeping tabs on me all along, though I doubt whether he'd admit it.'

'And you wouldn't have returned otherwise?'

'I'd been ordered never to darken his door again. It was up to him to make the first move. I wasn't going to beg.'

No, she thought. That had the authentic Benedict ring about it. And he'd come back for Austin, not for her. The thought stirred in her mind, causing a stab of pain, and was instantly stifled.

'I'm surprised you agreed at all.'

'On balance I had too much to lose.' He added almost casually, 'And some scores to settle.'

Lydie missed a step. 'I—see.'

'Not yet, perhaps,' Marius said easily, steadying her. 'But it's early days.'

Her heart lurched in fright. That, again, was almost a threat, she thought, swallowing. But why? She'd done nothing—except fall in love—with the wrong man—at the wrong time. He was the one who'd broken the rules—and her heart . . .

She was too close to him suddenly, his arm like a band of steel around her, the heat of his hard body warming the chill of her flesh, as if the layers of clothes between them had ceased to exist.

She said unevenly, 'People are changing partners now. You should dance with Mrs Mottram, our MP's wife. She's over there in the red dress.'

'How singularly inappropriate.' He made no attempt to release her. 'Let Jon do the honours—if he can tear himself away from the whisky for long enough.'

Damn him for noticing, she thought raggedly. And damn my idiot of a brother for providing him with an easy target.

She tried for nonchalance. 'He's had a trying day.'

'The first of many, I suspect,' he came back with equal smoothness.

Lydie bit her lip. 'Leave Jon alone,' she said. 'He's not up to your weight.'

'How charmingly protective,' Marius said softly. 'But that's what divides the human family from the animal kingdom. In the wild the weakest member of the pack is left for the predators.'

'With you, no doubt, as king of the jungle.'

The grey eyes glittered down at her. 'I'll settle for nothing less—Madonna Lily.'

All the breath seemed to catch in her throat. 'I told you—don't call me that.'

'No?' His voice was like silk. 'But it brings back so many delightful memories.'

'Not,' she said stonily, 'to me.'

'Then I'll have to jog your memory.'

For a searing second Lydie was pinned against him, her breasts crushed against the firm wall of his chest, his leg thrusting between hers in blatant eroticism as the last chords of the waltz died away. His breath fanned her cheek. His mouth grazed her ear. The unforgotten scent of his skin seemed to fill her senses.

Blood rushed into her face. 'Let go of me.' Her voice shook. 'How dare you...?'

He let her pull away, but retained hold of her hand as he escorted her from the floor, pausing to lift it to his lips in a mocking parody of a graceful courtesy, turning her fingers in his at the last moment so that his mouth stung her soft palm instead, swiftly and sensuously. Lethally.

He said quite gently, 'So you do remember after all.' And walked away.

She'd expected to find herself the embarrassed cynosure of dozens of pairs of avid eyes, but the only person who seemed to have registered what was going on was her mother.

Debra was staring at her, her brows drawn together, her teeth gnawing at her bottom lip. Then the music started again and she moved off with Hugh, laughing, chatting with apparent animation, hostess mask back in place.

Jon appeared at Lydie's side. 'What an enjoyable evening.' His speech was slightly slurred. 'All quiet on the united front.'

'Oh, shut up.' Lydie smiled through gritted teeth. 'Come and dance with me while you can still stand.'

'Is this permitted in the Th-Thornshaugh book of etiquette?' he asked plaintively. 'Brother and sister cavorting?'

'You'd better start reading survival manuals instead,' Lydie muttered. 'We all had.'

'Depends how badly you want to survive.' Jon peered round the marquee. 'I saw yet another old friend earlier putting on a brave face. Remember Nadine Winton?'

'Vividly,' Lydie said with a snap. 'I thought she was married and living in Surrey now.'

'Divorced, apparently, and back with the spoils of war, if the emeralds she's wearing are anything to go by.' He paused. 'Wasn't she walking out with Marius once upon a time?'

'Very much so,' Lydie agreed levelly.

'Maybe he can be persuaded to have another crack at her. Take his mind off his work. Give me time to sort out a few things.'

'Oh, God.' Lydie's heart sank. 'What sort of things?'

Jon shrugged. 'A few minor cock-ups. Nothing serious.'

'I hope not.' She touched the tip of her tongue to her lips. 'Jon, he's gunning for you already—'

'May I cut in?' enquired the jovial voice of the rural dean, and Lydie forced a smiling acquiescence.

And after that the party developed into a medley of faces and a blur of voices and laughter to which she made herself respond.

At one point, through the throng, she saw Marius dancing with the former Nadine Winton, a lusciously curved brunette.

Dear God, she thought, I used to be so jealous of her.

She watched Nadine smile up at him, sliding her hands up to his shoulders, the matching bracelets on her tanned wrists winking green fire, and realised, as pain stabbed through her, that nothing had changed. That seeing Marius with another woman still had the power to rip her apart.

Oh, dear God, no, it can't be true, she thought desperately. Then, more forcefully, I won't allow it to be true.

Hugh found her during the supper interval. 'I haven't been able to get near you all night,' he grumbled good-naturedly.

'Proves it's a good party.' She slid her arm through his, drawing it against her breast. My lifeline, she thought, her emotions churning. My saviour.

'Can I have your attention, everyone?' Debra was up on the bandstand, projecting charm. 'They say all good things come in threes. So far tonight we've had my husband's birthday—and Marius's homecoming. Now I understand there's going to be an announcement which will bring me—' her face was misty '—the greatest personal happiness.' She turned, reaching out both hands, all radiant spontaneity. 'Hugh, my dear, and Lydie, darling child, would you come up here?'

Lydie seemed to be staring at her mother's silver-clad figure down the wrong end of a telescope. She blinked, trying to get her into focus, to control her whirling thoughts.

'You don't mind, do you, sweetheart?' Hugh was whispering urgently. 'This was her idea, actually. I'd planned something a bit more private.'

Lydie found herself being propelled forward towards the bandstand.

Hugh was going to propose to her, she thought, dry-mouthed, in front of all these people. There'd be no going back after this. But why should she want to go back anyway? She'd be safe with Hugh... And safety— a refuge—was what she wanted—needed above all else.

She saw Jon smiling at her, lifting a wavering glass, his face conveying a blurred irony. And Austin, beside him, clutching a forbidden cigar, his face oddly set.

Saw Marius, standing as if he'd been chipped out of stone from the nearby moors, his eyes grey ice. Saw, as everyone else seemed to recede into some hazy distance, his lips move. Heard the silent words above the laughter and approving applause.

'Madonna Lily.'

She tore her hand free from Hugh's. Her voice was hoarse. 'I—I can't, you see.' She stared up at him wildly, willing him to understand. 'I thought I could—I wanted to. Please—please believe that...'

Her voice cracked, and she turned and ran, the stunned onlookers parting like the Red Sea, back to the uncertain peace of the house.

CHAPTER FOUR

THE party had been over for hours. From the window-seat in her room Lydie had heard the goodnights being called and watched the headlights departing. Now the house was quiet and in darkness.

She couldn't go to bed. She was too restless—too on edge. She'd started to undress, then abandoned the idea, throwing a robe over her teddy instead.

She'd half expected an irate visit from her mother, but presumably Debra had decided that it was too late for confrontations and was saving herself for a major scene in the morning.

Lydie shivered slightly. She'd brought it on herself. There were no excuses she could proffer, no apologies she could make.

She should never have allowed things to get that far with Hugh. She realised that now, when it was too late. She'd let the tide of events carry her along towards an engagement without allowing herself to examine her feelings and motives too closely. She'd accepted the view of Hugh as 'a good husband' without once asking herself if she'd make him an equally good wife.

That was quite bad enough. Now she'd publicly humiliated him, and ruined Austin's birthday party as well.

The indictment against her was building up.

She put her fingertips against her aching forehead. And it was Saturday tomorrow, one of their busiest days, and Nell would be expecting her in the gallery as usual at opening time. She had to make herself relax, get some

47

rest somehow, or she'd be fit for nothing. She'd try her usual remedy.

She thrust her bare feet into a pair of heel-less sandals and quietly opened her door. Not a sound anywhere.

Downstairs was a disaster area. First thing in the morning a local cleaning firm would arrive to remove the debris and restore Greystones to its usual pristine condition, chivvied by Mrs Arnthwaite.

Lydie wrinkled her nose at the sour smell of alcohol and tobacco smoke lingering in the air as she went through the big conservatory and into the pool-house beyond.

It had originally been another conservatory, but Austin had expanded it, retaining the elegant domed roof and replacing the walls with sliding glazed panels which could be pushed open in hot weather. Usually they remained closed, although tonight the evening had been warm.

Apart from a languid game of golf, swimming was Debra's only real exercise, and she kept the pool well heated.

As Lydie switched on the lamp at the door, she could see the gentle steam rising from the water.

The party had obviously extended into here, as it usually did. The loungers and wrought-iron tables and chairs around the edge were draped with damp and discarded towels. There was even a bucket containing the last remnants of some melting ice and a half-empty bottle of white wine.

At more optimistic moments she would have said it was half-full, Lydie thought wryly, finding an unused glass.

The wine was cold and dry, caressing her parched throat as she sipped it. The condemned woman drank a hearty breakfast, she thought with irony.

She put the glass back on the table, and dropped her robe to the floor. Still in her black silk teddy, she walked to the side of the pool and dived in with hardly a splash.

This was her usual panacea. She'd spent hours down here in the pool when the rest of the house was asleep. There was something about the movement of the water against her body which soothed her, driving the demons away.

A few lengths, and she'd be able to go back to her room and sleep. 'Perchance to dream'...?

No, she thought as she turned at the end of the pool and began to swim back. No dreams. Not tonight. She didn't want her rest tormented by any of those wantonly erotic images which left her stranded in a wilderness of aching frustration. And which always began in the same way—with the heavy, rich scent of lilies...

She turned onto her back and floated for a while, staring up into the darkness beyond the elaborate glass dome, her hair a pale cloud around her on the water.

She felt like a mermaid, some doomed half-woman of the deep, endlessly singing her siren songs to call a lover who didn't answer.

Who hadn't answered for five long years.

Then, suddenly, 'What the devil...?' It was Marius's voice, harsh with anger. The main lights in the poolhouse came on, dazzling her. She cried out. Her body jackknifed in shock, and for a moment she floundered, choking on the water she'd swallowed.

Dimly, she heard a splash, then he was beside her. 'It's all right. I've got you.'

Like hell he had. She kicked herself free and swam to the edge, resting an arm on the smooth turquoise tiles while she recovered her breath.

He joined her. 'Are you out of your mind?' he demanded hoarsely.

'Are you?' she countered. His dinner jacket was lying on the side where he'd dropped it. His black tie was floating on the water, and his elegant ruffled shirt was plastered against his body. He hadn't been to bed either, she thought. 'What are you doing here?'

'I took one of the guests home.' Marius pushed his wet hair out of his eyes. 'When I got back, I saw the light in here. I thought it had been left on by mistake. I came to the door, and I saw you in the water—not moving—your hair...'

One of the guests, she thought. She wasn't going to ask if it was Nadine. She didn't want to know.

She said coolly, 'I'm sorry if I startled you—'

'That's putting it mildly,' he cut in savagely.

'And naturally I'll pay for your dress suit to be cleaned,' she went on, raising her voice a notch. 'But your rescue attempt was quite unnecessary. I'm an excellent swimmer.'

'Do you make a habit of this? Coming down here alone at all hours?'

Lydie hunched a shoulder defensively. 'It's a free country.'

'But there are basic rules to be obeyed, nonetheless,' he said curtly. 'And you never swim, even in a pool this size, without someone knowing. It's much too easy to get into difficulties, especially when you've been drinking.' He threw a grim look at the wine bottle and glass. 'You drowning in the pool could be one sensation too many for this household,' he added pointedly.

Lydie groaned. 'Oh, God; was it terrible after I left?'

'I've known better moments.' Marius pulled himself out of the water and walked towards the changing cabin, unbuttoning his shirt. 'Your flight, by the way, was put down to pathological shyness triggering an incredibly early attack of bridal nerves.'

'That's ridiculous.'

'Well, there had to be some explanation.' Stripped down to black briefs, Marius began to towel himself vigorously. Wherever he'd been in the past years, there'd been no shortage of sun, she thought, her breath catching. He had a magnificent tan, his body as firm and muscular as ever... 'So let's hear yours.'

'I don't think I have one,' Lydie said, after a pause. He stopped, his brows lifting. 'You mean you just set that poor sod up then did a runner for the hell of it?'

'No, of course not.' She bit her lip.

'What, then?' The grey eyes were very cold and steady.

Because of you, she thought. You seduced me then walked away, without a word or a backward glance, leaving me with the knowledge that I hadn't been the only one. Without my being sure whether or not you had another illegitimate child on the way. And the reality of that's been crucifying me for five endless years.

And yet tonight, when I had the chance to put it behind me, all you had to do was look at me and I was lost. Nothing else mattered, least of all my sense of decency.

She shrugged again, the strap of her teddy sliding down from her shoulder. 'I simply realised I couldn't go through with it after all. Quite inexcusable, but a fact.' Her voice sounded clipped, brittle. 'I—I didn't bargain for it all being quite so public.' She swallowed. 'I expect everyone's disgusted with me. My—my mother will be so angry...'

'She was,' he returned dispassionately. 'But she calmed down considerably when my uncle pointed out that she was partly to blame for turning the whole thing into a three-ring circus.'

'Oh.' Lydie pushed herself away from the side and swam in a wide circle. 'He's very kind.'

'With a keen sense of justice.' Marius draped the towel he'd been using over a chair and shrugged on the robe he'd brought from the cabin. 'At least, what he sees to be justice.' His sudden smile was wintry. He picked up Lydie's own robe from the floor and held it out. 'It's time we called it a night.'

She grasped the handrail, pulling herself out of the water in one lithe movement, shivering as the chill of the air reached her.

She saw his eyes widen, and the sudden flare of colour along the high cheekbones as he looked at her. And she realised what he was seeing.

The soaked teddy was clinging to her, outlining her rounded breasts and the delicate nipples, hardened to prominence by cold and sudden excitement. The black silk hugged the flat plane of her stomach and the small hollow of her navel, and gave delicious emphasis to the gentle mound at the joining of her thighs.

She thought, I might as well be naked. And remembered his face—that first time—hunger mingled with a kind of reverence as he'd bent to kiss away the last remnants of shyness, warming her, bringing her to glowing, acquiescent life. To undreamed-of passion.

Now his face was a stranger's, the lines of his jaw taut, his mouth compressed. He looked older, tired, suddenly bitter.

She wanted to take his head between her hands and draw it to her breasts. To kiss his mouth, and eyes, and make him smile again. To make him, once more, the Marius who had loved her throughout that one unforgettable night with such completeness.

And then left her.

The thought jarred in her mind like a blow. That was what she mustn't forget. Not the loving, but the loneliness and bewilderment which had followed. The sense of utter betrayal. And all the unanswered questions about his departure that she still dared not ask this—stranger.

However much she might want to ask. However much, she thought with a shiver, she might want him. As she could no longer deny.

'Marius...' His name trembled into the silence between them, aching with bewilderment—with need. The tension, the longing was almost tangible, she realised, and surely mutual as well. Now—now he must reach for her...

She took one small, uncertain step towards him.

And saw his mouth twist in sudden mockery, his eyes flicking over her body in a sexual appraisal that was almost an insult.

He said softly, 'All in good time, beauty.' He threw the robe to her. 'Now cover yourself.' His voice seemed to reach her from a vast distance.

She huddled the robe on, fumbling with the sash, feeling the hot colour swamp her face.

She dredged up enough pride to say, 'Goodnight,' and turned to go.

'Goodnight.' His voice was cool, almost expressionless. 'And don't swim down here alone at night again. It isn't safe.'

She nodded, and went without looking back.

She thought, Nothing's safe now—nor ever will be again.

Sleep was still impossible. The room was like an oven, the mattress like a bed of nails. Lydie sat on the window-seat, drying her damp hair slowly and watching the sky for the first faint streaks of morning light.

She was shaken—appalled to realise that she'd allowed Marius a second opportunity to reject her. Oh, he'd wanted her, as his behaviour at the party had made clear, she thought bitterly. But he hadn't wanted her enough. The scornful indifference in his grey eyes made her tingle with shame in retrospect.

But then, she thought carefully, he'd never wanted her enough. Otherwise he wouldn't have left her. Would never have walked away.

Not that it should be allowed to matter any more. She had to sort herself out. What had happened to all her good intentions? she wondered wearily. She was like some human lemming, hell-bent on self-destruction.

And yet once, for a short while, she'd been so completely happy.

She couldn't remember exactly when she'd begun to love Marius. It had happened slowly, naturally over the years, like a rose taking root and putting out the first tender buds.

He'd taught her to ride, taken her walking over the high moors, talked to her—and listened in turn. In fact, he was the first person ever to be interested in her as a person. Heady stuff, she thought wryly.

And then, one day, as she'd hovered on the threshold between adolescence and womanhood, she'd looked at him and seen him for the dynamic, attractive male being he undoubtedly was.

She could even recall the exact moment. She'd been playing tennis and had cycled back to Greystones. Marius had been occupying a sun-lounger on the front lawn, wearing just a pair of ancient white shorts, and his skin had gleamed like bronze, his thick brown hair gilded at the ends by the sun.

Nadine Winton had been beside him. Lydie could remember dismounting from her bike with the intention of joining them. But she'd paused, sheltered by the tall shrubs which lined the drive, as Nadine had leaned across and kissed Marius on the mouth. Lydie had seen her hand with its scarlet-tipped nails tracing patterns on the hair-roughened skin of his chest, then sliding down deliberately over his abdomen—like some pale, exotic snake, Lydie had thought from where she stood.

She'd felt hot with sudden embarrassment, yet cold as ice at the same time. She'd wanted to run away, but she'd been rooted to the spot, a strange, shamed warmth uncurling in the pit of her stomach. She'd seen Nadine's other hand lift to unhook her bikini top and let it fall away.

Lydie left her bike where it was and crept indoors and upstairs. She'd taken a long shower, letting the water cascade over her. Then, wrapped in a towel, she'd come back into her room.

There was a long mirror on the wall, and she let the towel drop to the floor and for the first time in her life scrutinised her naked body as something more than the frame she fed and hung clothes on. For once she tried to appraise herself as the object of a man's desire, the centre of his pleasure.

But not just any man. It was Marius whom she wanted to see her like this, as she twisted and turned, running tentative hands over her blossoming breasts, her slender flanks, and the slight concavity of her belly. It was Marius she wanted to kiss her and to touch her. To do to her the secret things that instinct told her he and Nadine were engaged in at that moment, their loungers deserted now in the drowsy heat.

The realisation made her gasp, her arms wrapping in self-protection across her body as pain consumed her.

In the past, Marius's girlfriends had been a source of half-tolerant, half-scornful amusement. Now everything had changed and they were bitter rivals.

And she knew, with a kind of sadness, that her relationship with Marius had changed for ever too. That the old ease and trust would be replaced by something else—something altogether less comfortable, which might bring either reward or heartbreak in its wake.

And she thought, I'll make him want me. I'll make him love me.

Almost at once, she began to distance herself from him in all kinds of tiny ways, divorcing herself from the old camaraderie, forcing him to be aware of her in a totally different fashion, but careful not to overdo it. 'One charmer... is quite enough': his words which she'd never forgotten.

One evening after dinner, they were all in the drawing room listening to music. It was Rachmaninov—sweeping, romantic and poignant—and she was sitting on the rug in front of the fireplace, lost in her own private world of fantasy and longing, unaware when the compact disc reached its end.

'And where were you, then?' Austin asked her jovially. He looked round with a grin. 'I think the lass must be in love.'

He teased her broadly about the unknown boyfriend, Jon joining in, building up a ludicrous picture of a cross between Rupert Brooke, whose poems she'd been studying at school, and Arnold Schwarzenegger. And in the middle of all the hilarity she saw Marius looking at her, mouth set and brows drawn together, as if he'd been totally arrested by some new and not completely welcome possibility.

From then on they shared a strange new awareness of each other. On the surface everything appeared to be the same, but Marius was careful, she noticed, never to be alone with her, as if some fragile truce existed between them that the intimacy of a private word or a look could shatter.

As if they were both waiting for some special moment, she mused now, as she sat anticipating the first light of dawn irradiating the eastern sky.

Waiting, she thought, for her to grow up. To come of age in years as well as mind and body.

It had been Christmas and she had just turned seventeen when everything changed irrevocably. There'd been a party at Greystones for some of Austin's friends, and Debra had insisted that Lydie attend to hand round food and behave like the daughter of the house.

Marius had had other parties to go to, and, to Debra's fury, he'd taken Jon with him. Austin had shrugged at her complaints.

'They're young men—bachelors,' he told her with a touch of impatience. 'Naturally they'll be in demand. You've got the lass tied to your apron strings. Be content with that, my dear.'

They came back around midnight. Lydie was just going through the hall to tell Mrs Arnthwaite to serve the mulled wine when the front door opened on an icy shaft of wind and Jon came in laughing uproariously, with Marius just behind him.

'Look at this.' Jon pointed to a few melting flakes of white adhering to his coat. 'It's going to be a white Christmas.' He picked Lydie up and swung her round, then abandoned her, making for the drawing room and the buzz of laughter and conversation.

Marius took off his overcoat and dropped it onto the big carved settle. He looked at Lydie, then glanced upwards, an odd smile twisting his mouth. Lydie followed the direction of his gaze and saw that Jon had put her down under the big mistletoe garland hanging from the ceiling.

A feeling rather like panic gripped her throat. Maybe she should move away. Maybe...

Marius reached her. His hands took her shoulders, drawing her towards him very gently. He said softly, 'Merry Christmas,' and bent his head to kiss her on the mouth.

The touch of his lips on hers lit a small, wild flame inside her. She kissed him back, all the feelings she'd repressed for so long feeding the innocent fire of her lips, turning it to a sudden conflagration.

She heard Marius groan in his throat. His hands tightened on her, pulling her against him. She felt the slam of his heart through the wool shirt, and the stroke of his fingers exploring the slender length of her spine.

Her mouth parted under the pressure of his, willingly, eagerly. His tongue was heated satin against hers as she responded almost mindlessly to the deepening demand of his kiss.

They were clinging together, bodies locked and straining, oblivious to everything but the moment, drinking—breathing each other.

Debra's acid 'What in the world is going on?' brought them plummeting back to reality.

She was standing in the drawing-room doorway, her face like ice.

She said, 'May I remind you, Lydie, that we have guests? And that you're rather young to be receiving drunken advances, even with Christmas as an excuse?'

Marius half turned towards her, his arm still clamped round Lydie. He said, too quietly, 'I'm not drunk. Nor do I need an excuse.'

Their glances met in challenge, and it was Debra who turned away first. She said coldly, 'Lydie, I sent you on an errand,' then went back into the drawing room and closed the door.

'You'd better do as she tells you,' Marius muttered ruefully. He paused. 'At least for the time being.'

His hand stroked her cheek and she turned her head, almost blindly, consumed by joy at the promise she heard—or seemed to hear—in his words, pressing her lips to his fingers in a fleeting caress.

Then, suddenly shy, she disengaged herself and ran off to tell Mrs Arnthwaite about the mulled wine.

She didn't go back to the drawing room immediately. She let herself out by the side-door into the garden.

The snow was falling quite heavily, the tiny flakes whirling in the floodlights which illumined the house, covering the shrubbery and lawns with a frosting of magic.

Lydie lifted her face, laughing at their feather-like touch against her skin, too excited to feel cold.

He's mine, she thought exultantly as the snow pearled to moisture on her face. Mine at last—and for ever.

There were other drops on her face now, in this pre-dawn hush, salt and scalding as they rolled down her cheeks, unbidden and unchecked, reminding her once more, with cruel emphasis, just how wrong she'd been.

CHAPTER FIVE

'YOU must be quite mad,' Debra Benedict said angrily, 'turning down an opportunity like that.'

Lydie noted wryly that her mother had referred to Hugh as an opportunity rather than a person. She said patiently, 'I wasn't in love with him.'

Debra laughed harshly. 'A fine time to discover that.'

'Better now, surely, than after we were married?' Lydie felt weary. Austin might have taken her mother to task the previous night, but she'd had time to build up her resentment all over again.

'Hugh could have made you happy,' Debra said intensely. 'You'd have had everything—money, social position, the Wingate name...' She cast her eyes to heaven. 'And you drivel on about sentimental rubbish. I doubt now whether he'll ever speak to you again.'

'Then I shall miss his friendship,' Lydie said quietly.

'And Jon's almost as bad.' Debra petulantly hitched up a pillow. 'Both of you—throwing your futures away with both hands. You know he passed out last night, I suppose? That—creature took charge—made sure he was put to bed. He must be laughing up his sleeve this morning.'

'I presume the "creature" is Marius,' Lydie remarked evenly. 'I think you'll have to make up your mind that he's back for good, Mama, and learn to be civil.'

Debra's hands picked restlessly at the tissue she was holding, reducing it to shreds. 'I can't believe it's happened—that Austin's actually allowed him back here. I thought we were rid of him for good. But it's all been for nothing.'

Lydie stared at her in shock. There was real venom in her mother's voice. It was like watching a veneer being peeled back, she thought, and finding something corrupt and corrosive underneath.

She said levelly, 'It might be wiser to try and be glad for Austin that they've made up their—quarrel.' She paused painfully. 'That he's decided to forgive and forget after all.'

'Don't talk like a fool.' Debra dealt forcefully with the voice of reason. 'I haven't sacrificed the past few years to this dead-and-alive hole just to see my plans fall to pieces now.'

She dusted the remains of the tissue off her hands with a fastidious grimace. 'But there's no point in talking to you. Aren't you supposed to be at your pathetic little gallery?'

'I am indeed,' Lydie agreed.

Her thoughts were sombre as she went downstairs. Lack of sleep had left her feeling hollow, and her eyes felt bruised.

She was also seriously disturbed and alarmed by the way her mother had spoken. She'd always thought that Debra Benedict's eye to the main chance had been leavened by genuine affection for Austin, but now she wasn't so sure.

I don't understand any of it, she thought. I don't know what's going on any more—if I ever did.

She could hear the rumble of Austin's bass coming from the dining room, interspersed with Marius's lighter drawl. She'd have sold her soul for a cup of coffee but she couldn't risk another confrontation, not when she was physically and emotionally at such a low ebb.

She'd wept last night until her eyes and throat had felt raw, but it had exorcised none of her demons.

She was beginning to realise the implications of sharing a roof with Marius again—of lying alone and awake each night, aching for him.

And it was useless to tell herself that she was a fool who should have more self-respect. She had to deal with matters as they were, and not as how she might prefer them to be.

Marius had returned, so she would have to leave. It was as simple as that.

It was a day brilliant with sunshine, and the tourists were out in force, including a heaven-sent bus-load of Americans. Business at the gallery was brisk, leaving Lydie only enough time to give Nell a heavily edited run-down on events at the party, and no opportunity to lose herself in more painful reverie. For which she could only be grateful.

During a brief lull, Lydie dashed to the local sandwich shop for their lunch. On her return, she found Nell on her knees, looking through a portfolio.

'What have you got there?'

'The most extraordinary thing.' Nell's face was rapt. 'A girl just walked in off the street and asked if we could sell these watercolours for her. Look.'

Lydie looked, her lips pursing into a whistle of astonished delight. 'My God, she's good. Is she from round here? Why haven't we heard about her before?'

'I wish I knew. She's young and a bit aggressive, with traces of a local accent.' Nell examined the label attached to the portfolio. 'Darrell Corbin,' she read. 'Quarry Row. I don't even know where that is.'

'I do.' Lydie frowned faintly. 'But I didn't know anyone still lived there. The quarry's been closed for years.'

'Maybe you could call in there,' Nell suggested. 'Tell her we'd love to handle her work. See what you can find out about her. She wasn't very forthcoming with me.'

'I'll pop in this evening on my way home.'

Anything that kept her away from Greystones at the moment was a bonus, Lydie thought ruefully. And this new artist was a find worth cultivating.

The portfolio contained mainly local scenes, using the watercolour medium with a strong, sure touch. Darrell Corbin seemed particularly drawn to the high moors, revealing how sunlight and the play of cloud could change the landscape from windswept romanticism to a brooding, almost sinister intensity.

While Nell made coffee to go with their sandwiches, Lydie hunted round the till area.

'Have you seen the local paper?'

'I used it to wrap those ceramic goblets,' Nell admitted. 'They were going all the way to Ohio. Did you want it for anything special?'

Lydie bit her lip. 'I was going to see what was available under "Flats to Rent",' she returned with studied lightness.

Nell nearly choked on her coffee. 'You're leaving Greystones?' She shook her head. 'I don't believe it.'

Lydie shrugged. 'We all have to move on some time.'

'Some of us do,' Nell agreed drily. 'Some don't.'

Lydie knew that she meant Jon. She hadn't told her about his behaviour at the party, because Nell thought he drank too much anyway.

Nell eyed her. 'Could this surge of independence have anything to do with yesterday's return of the native?'

'It might.' Lydie avoided her look.

Nell blessedly didn't probe any further, merely handing her a beaker of coffee. 'Well, you can always move in with me,' she offered matter-of-factly.

'I know.' Lydie was genuinely touched. Nell's living space comprised barely enough room to swing a gerbil. 'But where would you put me?'

'I could always empty the fridge.' Nell patted her shoulder. 'Anyway, the offer's there.' She glanced towards the gallery door. 'And here come some more customers. They must have smelt the coffee.'

By the end of the afternoon, they'd sold four of Darrell Corbin's unframed watercolours, all at good prices. 'An investment,' Nell had told the buyers, and meant it. 'She's a name of the future.'

Nell looked at her watch. 'I need to pop to the supermarket before it closes. Can you close up here?' She handed Lydie a slip of paper. 'That's what we owe Darrell Corbin already. Maybe you could take her a cheque—spur her to more activity?'

'Glad to.' Lydie wondered if Nell would be seeing Jon over the weekend, but decided it was more tactful not to ask. They had to work out their own problems, she thought with a sigh. And so did she.

She lingered after Nell's precipitate departure, relishing the quiet of the gallery after the day's bustle. She wrote the cheque for Darrell Corbin, and had paused briefly on her way out, to tidy a display of wooden figures, when the jangle of the shop bell made her jump.

'I'm sorry, we're closed—' she began, and stopped as she realised who the late caller was.

'I realise that.' Marius strolled forward. He was wearing light trousers and a shirt the colour of old copper. They looked Italian and expensive, Lydie thought, her throat tightening uncontrollably at the sight of him.

He took a long, slow look around. 'You have some good stuff here,' he remarked. 'Austin liked his present.'

She said tautly, 'I'm glad.' Then, 'I didn't know you were interested in arts and crafts.'

'I'm not as a general rule.' He paused. 'But I've spent the day going through some of the financial statements with Austin, and I regard this place almost as a Benco subsidiary.'

He spoke pleasantly, but the words found their target.

Faint colour rose in Lydie's face, and warning bells sounded. She said quietly, 'I understood the loan was a private matter between Austin and myself.'

'It was, but I shall be handling the family finances from now on, as well as the company business.'

'I—see. I—I didn't know that.' She tried to keep her dismay out of her voice, imagining her mother's reaction.

'No one else does,' he said. 'Austin's decided to take his retirement very seriously indeed.'

'I'm glad about that too. But you didn't have to make a special journey to tell me.'

'True.' The grey eyes met hers without expression. 'Actually, I thought we might have dinner together.'

Lydie replaced the last wooden figure with infinite care. 'Now, why should I want to do that?' Her heart was bumping against her ribs, but she kept her voice steady.

'Because you might find it marginally preferable to eating at home.' He paused. 'Your mother has invited Hugh Wingate.'

'What?' She almost shrieked the word. 'Oh, I don't believe it.'

'Ring home. Check.'

'What's the point?' Lydie raised clenched fists towards the ceiling. 'She knows the score—I told her this morning. How could she do such a thing?'

'Your mother takes the single-minded viewpoint—her own.' Marius sounded cool and faintly bored. 'I hear there's a good Italian place opened on the other side of the valley.'

'Yes, but it's always heaving on Saturday. You need to book,' she said curtly, still fuming over Debra's high-handedness.

'I already have,' he said.

That arrested her attention. She lifted her chin. 'You were so sure I'd come with you?'

'Not at all.' A faint smile softened the harsh lines of his mouth. 'You may well prefer to go back to Greystones and listen to Wingate being magnanimous. Forgive me if I don't join you.'

She'd rather be boiled in oil and they both knew it, but even if she refused he wouldn't be short of company at his table for two, she thought. Nadine Winton was probably sitting by the phone at that very moment, willing it to ring.

She squashed down a shaft of ignoble triumph. She had nothing at all to be pleased about. She was simply risking more heartbreak, more torment by allowing herself to be even marginally involved with Marius again. She would have done far better to have invented an alternative engagement. But his comments about the gallery were still niggling in her mind. Maybe it was better not to antagonise him unnecessarily.

She picked up her bag, stuffing Darrell Corbin's cheque into its side-pocket. That would have to wait.

'I'll have to get my car from the yard or it'll be locked up for the rest of the weekend,' she said as she fastened the gallery door.

'Leave it at the mill instead.'

'I'm honoured,' she threw over her shoulder. 'Can I use the managing director's spot?'

He shrugged. 'Why not?'

'Because in the past the mill's always seemed like hallowed ground. I've never felt welcome to set foot there.'

'Perhaps you've never convinced anyone that you're interested in doing a serious job. It's not a playground.'

Ouch, Lydie thought grimly. That puts me in my place.

She said with a touch of acid, 'Is that how you see the gallery—as a kind of toy?'

'I need to see your time sheets before judging your level of commitment,' Marius said softly. 'But few people trying to get a business off the ground in its first year can allow themselves nearly three weeks' holiday.'

He'd learned a lot during his day with the financial statements, she thought shakily.

She said, 'The arrangements had all been made in advance. I couldn't really get out of them—and Nell understood.'

He nodded. 'Does she get much time to do her own painting these days?' he asked. 'I hear she used to be good.'

What hadn't he heard?

Lydie lifted her chin. 'As far as I'm aware, she still is,' she said.

Why didn't he come straight out with it and call her a spoiled, selfish bitch? she asked herself angrily. But that had never been Marius's way. He simply cast his line and left you wriggling on the hook.

And Nell had never complained about the amount of time she'd had off. But then Nell wouldn't, she acknowledged ruefully.

She said tartly, 'I hope you're not going to walk into Benco and start making snap judgements.'

'I don't need to,' he said. 'I'm already well aware of the problems. I thought long and hard before coming back here, believe me.' He flicked a glance at her.

'Although there were personal incentives,' he added silkily.

There was a tingling silence. For a moment, she was tempted to cancel dinner, go back to Greystones and face whatever music was playing there.

She heard him laugh softly. His hand took her arm, gently but very firmly. He said calmly, as if she'd spoken aloud, 'Forget it, Lydie. You're better off where you are. Now, let's get your car.'

His own vehicle was just as amazing as Jon had implied—sleek, streamlined and reeking of concealed power. Lydie sank into the passenger seat, breathing in the fragrance of the leather upholstery. Her workaday skirt and shirt felt positively shabby in contrast, she thought with vexation.

'I didn't realise we'd be travelling in such style.' She stole a sideways glance at him. 'I'm glad to know you haven't been begging in the streets.'

'Begging isn't my scene,' he said.

No, she thought. It never had been. Marius reached out and took what he wanted—and suffered the consequences . . .

She drew a deep breath. 'Where did you go?'

'Here and there.' He didn't prevaricate by asking what she meant, but he wasn't giving much away either. 'I'd had a number of feelers from other companies during my Benco days. I decided to see which were genuine.'

'And they all were?'

'Most of them.'

She didn't doubt it. He'd always been the lad with the golden touch. Even the hard-headed local businessmen had agreed as much.

'So, where were you head-hunted to?' She kept her tone light, casually interested. 'Another textile firm?'

'No, the Kent subsidiary of an American company,' he said. 'After six months I was transferred to Boston. I travelled a lot after that—Mexico, South America. Last year I spent in Australia.'

Not just an ocean away, she thought, but the other side of the world. No wonder he hadn't responded when she'd tried to reach out to him during all those sleepless nights.

'And now you're here again.' She looked out at the steep street lined with terraced houses as the car climbed its way smoothly. 'This valley must seem very small and cramped after all those wide open spaces.'

'It's a question of belonging.'

So, where does that leave me? she wondered. In a furnished flat in some London suburb?

'And that's why you came back?'

'Partly.' She saw his mouth tighten. 'I didn't actually leave of my own accord, if you recall.'

I wish I could forget. She bit the words back, leaning forward as they came out onto the high road above the town. 'I think Topo Gigio's the other way.'

'Our table's booked for eight. I thought we'd have a drink first.'

'Oh,' she said.

'Is there anywhere you want to avoid?' His smile was pleasant. 'Did you use a particular pub with Hugh?'

Her mind went blank. Offhand, to her shame, she couldn't remember a single place where Hugh had taken her. 'Er—not really.'

The Three Horseshoes was old, and almost as rugged as the hillside it was built out from.

She remembered it at once as the place where Marius used to bring her after their walks over the moors.

She'd never been back since, but she could recall with mouth-watering accuracy the taste of the home-roast ham and the freshly baked teacakes he'd ordered—'to keep your strength up', he'd told her, laughing. But nothing stronger than orange juice to drink, in spite of her wheedling.

Inside, it was like stepping into a time-warp. There were a few more horse brasses on the dark beams and chimney breast, but everything else seemed unchanged. It was even the same landlord, albeit rather more grizzled.

While Marius ordered the drinks, Lydie did some frenzied repairs with comb, blusher and lipstick in the ladies' cloakroom. Her eyes were enormous, she thought with dissatisfaction, and her cheekbones looked like razor blades.

Her mother had thought that she was crazy for breaking up with Hugh. But this—this was real insanity, she told herself, stroking the fragrance of Dior's Dune on the pulse-points at her throat and wrists.

She thought, I should not be here.

When she arrived back in the bar, Marius handed her a glass of orange juice. 'For old times' sake,' he told her laconically. 'You can have a real drink later.'

She forced a smile in return, her throat constricting. 'Old times' sake'. Old times that were over for ever. Did he really think she needed a reminder of those late summer days when he'd taught her the beauty of the high moors—taught her to love the lonely rocks, the cry of the curlew, and the great sweep of wind-driven cloud which was never far away?

Or was he just being cruel? Lydie wondered bleakly as they took their drinks over to a table beside the inglenook. Was he punishing her for having stayed in his home-place while he was in exile?

But I'd have gone with him, she thought, biting her lip. In spite of everything, all he had to do was ask—

send for me, and I'd have been there. But there was nothing—nothing . . .

She was acutely conscious of him beside her on the worn, velvet-cushioned bench, of the brush of his thigh against hers.

She lifted her glass in a parody of a toast. 'Well—this is—kind of you,' she said stiltedly.

He stared at her. 'What the hell's kindness got to do with it?'

'You've rescued me from an awkward situation. And there must be so much else you could be doing tonight. So many other people to catch up with after all this time.' She was aware that she was babbling and stopped abruptly.

'At the moment,' he said, 'I'm catching up with you.'

She looked down at the table. 'I haven't moved very far.'

'No,' he said. 'And I'm wondering why not. You're a bright girl. You don't have to limit yourself to what Thornshaugh has to offer.'

'Nor do you.'

'Touché,' he said wryly. 'But I always knew I'd have people depending on me—relying on me to safeguard their livelihoods. That makes a difference.'

Her heart skipped a beat. Was he talking about the workforce, or more personal responsibilities? She realised she didn't want to know.

She hurried into speech again. 'It's the same for me now, in a way. The gallery's providing an outlet for local artists—for creative people in the area generally—helping them find their feet and start to sell their work. That has its own importance.'

'But you could have done that anywhere,' he said.

She shrugged. 'Nell likes Thornshaugh,' she said. 'She thinks it has potential.'

And I would never have gone away, she thought. Because all this time, God help me, I've been waiting—hoping that you'd come back.

'And what about your own creativity?' He lifted a hand and slowly stroked a strand of hair back form her forehead. 'How do you propose to channel that?'

Her breath quickened. She wanted to pull away, but at the same time was reluctant to let the casual caress assume too much importance.

'Oh, I'm the business end of the partnership,' she said, trying to laugh. 'I pay the bills and sweet-talk the bank manager.'

'God help him,' he said, an odd note in his voice. 'You could persuade anyone to do anything against his better judgement, Madonna Lily.'

Lydie looked away. 'Please don't call me that,' she said raggedly.

'Does it disturb you so much—even after all this long time?'

His fingers captured her chin, making her face him.

Eternity would make no difference, she thought achingly.

'I didn't say it disturbed me.' This time she pushed his hand away.

'Then why are you trembling?' he questioned softly.

'Hunger, I expect.' She pinned on a smile. 'We were too busy to eat our lunch today.'

For a moment he looked astonished, then he laughed. 'I never thought of that. Finish your drink, then, beauty, and I'll feed you.'

The cool grey gaze held hers. 'And then,' he added gently, 'we'll decide what to do for the rest of the evening. Agreed?'

In a voice she barely recognised, Lydie heard herself say, 'Yes.' And wondered exactly what she'd agreed to.

CHAPTER SIX

THEY had a corner table, candlelit and secluded, in a long, low room where most of the tables seemed to be for couples. Carved wooden columns supported the ceiling, garlanded by swathes of dried hops. French windows opening onto a terrace bright with flowering tubs took advantage of the late June evening.

They drank Frascati and shared a huge platter of Mediterranean prawns grilled with garlic butter and lemon juice, followed by chicken in a sauce thick with tomatoes and peppers. A girl with long hair and wistful eyes played the mandolin and sang in a sweet, high voice.

Lydie said, 'She's good,' and Marius agreed. 'And I like the decor,' she added. The walls had been rough-plastered and painted off-white. The table linen was in shades of deep amber and terracotta. 'Except for the candle-holders.' She touched one with a critical finger. 'We have some far nicer ones at the gallery. Perhaps I can do a deal.'

'Some other time,' he said. 'I want you to forget business completely tonight and concentrate wholly on pleasure.'

She pretended to be scandalised to cover the faint, dangerous flush of awareness warming her face. She let her lashes sweep down to veil her eyes in case they betrayed too much. She said hurriedly, trying to make a joke of it, 'But we're a Benco subsidiary now. We have to try harder.'

His eyes met hers. He said softly, 'When you look like that, Madonna Lily, you don't have to try at all.'

Her flush deepened uncontrollably. She was burning up—consumed by a flame which had nothing to do with embarrassment.

'But I forgot,' he went on. 'You don't like to be called that any longer. Tell me, have you reached the right age for Lydia yet?'

She recalled telling him once that when she'd been a small child she hadn't been able to manage the extra syllable on her name.

'And now I prefer Lydie anyway,' she added. 'Maybe one day I'll be grown-up enough for the sophisticated version.'

She'd known exactly when that would be—on the day she stood beside him in the parish church at Thornshaugh. I Lydia Catherine take thee Marius...

How simple it had all seemed then. How inevitable.

She said slowly, 'Fancy you remembering that.'

'I've forgotten very little.'

On the surface it was a commonplace remark, yet some faint discord set alarm bells jangling along Lydie's nerve-endings.

She had to be careful, she reminded herself. She couldn't allow herself to be seduced by the charm of their surroundings, and the stealthy, dangerous glow that his company always engendered.

She couldn't afford to forget, either, exactly what Marius had done to her.

She sent him a wary glance, but his attention seemed to be absorbed in refilling their glasses.

She said, with a slight shrug, 'Anyway, I haven't got to the Lydia stage yet. I seem to be stuck with the revised version.'

Marius lifted his glass, studying the colour of the wine. He said lightly, 'I confess it was a surprise to come back and find you hadn't changed your name even more fundamentally. I'd expected to find you married.'

Her heartbeat quickened. 'I suppose I could say the same for you.' She managed a small laugh. 'Or have you got a wife or something hidden away somewhere?'

The grey eyes watched her meditatively.

'No wife,' he said. 'Or anything.'

'No encumbrances of any kind?' She exaggerated the words, opening her eyes wide in a parody of curiosity, trying to hide the fact that her questions were in deadly earnest.

It was his turn to shrug. 'You know the saying—he travels fastest who travels alone.'

But there was someone, she thought. A girl who existed like a shadow in her mind, an image without a name or even a face. A girl who'd also lain in his arms and responded to the rapture of his lovemaking. A girl who'd found herself equally abandoned when Marius had gone away, but who had, at least, had his baby.

Whereas I, she thought, was left with no one and nothing.

There was a sudden tightness in her throat. Her appetite had gone, and she pushed her plate away.

'Is something wrong?'

'Not a thing.' She kept her voice light and bright. 'I simply can't eat any more.'

'No pudding?'

'Heavens, no.' She forced a giggle. 'I have to watch my figure.'

'If we're talking in clichés,' Marius said sardonically, 'I suppose I should say that's a pleasure you can safely leave to me.'

Lydie pulled a face. 'Oh, please. I wasn't looking for compliments—however trite.'

'I know that.' She felt her flush deepening as the searching grey glance swept over her again. 'You were a lovely child, Lydie. Now you're a beautiful woman.'

His voice was serious, his face unsmiling, as if the words had been forced from him against his will.

He had called her beautiful five years ago, she remembered with equal reluctance, his voice raw and shaking as he'd caressed her, all the barriers he'd built against the world torn away.

One flesh, she thought. That night we became one flesh. I thought they were just words. That it couldn't really happen. But it was true—the ultimate miracle. The two of us united—inseparable.

Now the man who'd taught her such complete abandon was a guarded stranger again, taking refuge behind a wall of silence and evasion.

Talk to me, she called to him silently. Tell me what happened. I have to know.

In the end Marius ordered fresh fruit for their dessert. They ate nectarines and dark plums with flesh as golden and sweet as honey. Lydie licked the juice from her lips and heard his swift intake of breath—saw the grey eyes sharpen to a new intensity, move from her mouth to the thrust of her breasts under her shirt.

Suddenly, she was aware that her nipples were hardening against the thin fabric in a response she could neither deny nor, seemingly, resist.

And she was watching him in turn. Looking at his hands as they moved to emphasise a point he'd just made, or held the stem of his glass, and imagined them— *remembered* them touching her, the long fingers tender against her skin, moving slowly, sensuously...

She thought in a kind of panic, Dear God, what's happening to me?

She should not be here with him, and she knew it. She'd have been safer at Greystones, enduring Hugh's wounded looks and unspoken reproaches.

She felt as if she was being enfolded in some invisible web of memory and secret, dark delight, drawn down some path where she knew she should not venture.

She should make some excuse, she knew. Tell him she had to leave—say anything...

But she said nothing. Just sat there as the enchantment gathered her up—intensified as the ache of yearning, so long subdued, diffused into sharper, more potent emotion, as the only reality became her own passionate need.

The meal drew to its leisurely conclusion, the waiter bringing coffee, and Sambucca, the coffee beans burning with a vivid blue flame in the tiny glasses.

They were among the last to leave. When the waiter brought the bill, he handed Lydie a flower—a carnation in deep clove-pink.

'Oh, how lovely.' She inhaled its scent, brushing the petals against her mouth.

Marius said softly, 'Lovely, indeed.' But he wasn't looking at the flower.

She felt a long quiver of guilty excitement tremble through her body. She was frightened, yet at the same time exultant. She reached for her bag, but emotion made her clumsy and she knocked it to the ground, the contents spilling out onto the flagged floor.

'Ah, *signorina*.' The waiter knelt, and so did Marius helping her pick things up. 'I hope your mirror not break.' He passed over her compact. 'No seven years' bad luck for you.'

It was intact. And I think, she whispered inwardly, that my luck could be on the turn.

'This was under the chair.' Marius was holding out Darrell Corbin's cheque.

'Oh, heavens, was it?' That was appalling carelessness, she berated herself, flushing, as she zipped the cheque into an inside pocket this time for safe-keeping.

There was a silence, then he said, 'I'll get the car.'

That was all he said, but she knew quite suddenly and definitely that something had changed.

She stared after him, watching his tall figure stride to the door and disappear, and she wanted to run after him, even though the car park was only about fifty yards away.

Instead, she fastened her bag, then followed Marius without haste, smiling her thanks at the waiter as she left.

She was a girl who'd had a wonderful meal, she thought with quiet detachment. In fact, a wonderful evening which was suddenly, and inexplicably, over.

The night breeze struck a chill through her shirt as she waited. She heard the impatient growl of the engine and saw the car's headlights approach, like great golden eyes seeking her in the darkness.

Marius opened the passenger door and she ran round and climbed in beside him. A tape was playing. Music to shelter behind, she thought; to make conversation unnecessary. This was the old Marius once more, with all the barriers firmly in place.

She was trembling again, but not, this time, with anticipation or pleasure.

She wanted to scream at him at the top of her voice, Don't do this to me, but instead she said, deliberately casual, 'That's a terrific place.'

'Yes, Nadine was quite right about it.' His reply was like a slap across the face. And a deliberate one, she was sure, reminding her that she was not, and never had been, the only one in his life.

As if she needed any such reminder.

She didn't venture any more remarks, just sat, rigidly, her mind churning, as the car ate up the miles back to Greystones.

He stopped outside the front door. He said courteously, 'If you'd like to get out, Lydie, I'll put the car away.'

'Yes, of course.' She fumbled with the seat belt, and with a barely repressed sigh he leaned across and released it for her. A breath of his cologne reached her—the old sharp, musky fragrance, totally personal, instantly recognisable.

She turned and put her lips softly and fleetingly to his cheek. Felt him tense—almost flinch at the brief contact. And could have wept.

She said calmly and sedately, 'Goodnight, Marius. And—thank you.'

'My pleasure.' His voice was cool, noncommittal.

She watched the car's tail-lights vanish, then went into the house alone.

Not again, Lydie thought as she paced restlessly up and down her bedroom carpet. This couldn't be happening again. She pressed her hands to her hot cheeks.

One moment she'd seemed so close to Marius, wrapped in an intimacy which had been almost tangible, the next, banished to some kind of outer darkness, without a word of explanation or regret. The misery of the last five years resurfaced in microcosm.

But she wasn't going to submit tamely to having her emotions ripped to shreds all over again, she thought rawly. This time she was going to find out exactly what game he'd been playing all evening.

But tonight was only part of it, of course. All the other unanswered questions still lay below the surface of her consciousness, savage and corrosive. However painful it might prove, this time she was going to demand the whole truth.

It seemed hours before he came upstairs. Straining her ears, she could hear the murmur of conversation as he said goodnight to Austin.

She sat tensely on the edge of the bed in her robe and nightgown, and waited. Downstairs, she heard a clock chime one. Otherwise the house seemed dark and silent.

She'd waited like this once before...

Quietly she let herself out of her room and trod barefoot down the passage to Marius's room. A crack of light still showed under the door, so at least he wasn't asleep—he was probably reading in bed.

She turned the handle gently and slipped into the room. The bed was certainly turned down ready for him, but the room was empty, and she stood for a moment, her mind a blank, feeling a little foolish, until her attention was alerted by the sound of the shower running from the adjacent bathroom.

Lydie hesitated. Maybe it would be better to postpone any confrontation until daylight after all, she thought, her eyes travelling reluctantly round the room.

It was barely recognisable now as her one-time sanctuary. Her mother's flair for interior decoration had ruthlessly stripped away every trace of Marius's presence. New wallpaper, curtains and bedcover had transformed it into just another anonymous spare room—exactly as Debra had intended, presumably.

Even the old brass bedstead had been got rid of, and there was no hiding place under the wide modern divan which had taken its place, however much she might suddenly feel the need of one, she thought wryly.

The only thing that hadn't changed was the scent of lilies flooding in through the open window from the garden below, exquisite and evocative in the same measure.

She thought, I definitely should not be here. But as she turned to go the bathroom door swung open and Marius emerged, his brown hair curling with damp, a towel draped casually round his hips.

He stopped dead when he saw her, his expression hardening to stone.

'What are you doing here?'

I couldn't stay away. That was what she'd said the last time he'd asked her that question in this room. Then she'd unfastened her dressing gown and let it fall to the floor, watching the grey eyes warm to slow, unquenchable flame as he absorbed every inch of her young, naked beauty.

But that wouldn't happen this time. The glitter in Marius's eyes was more like ice.

But then—that first time—that only time—she'd been so sure of him and his desire for her—his love...

Whereas this time—tonight—she wasn't sure of a thing—except that she'd been a fool to come here.

'Answer me, damn you,' he said harshly. 'Why are you here?'

Lydie lifted her chin. 'I want to know what happened tonight.'

'I thought we had an excellent meal in enjoyable surroundings.'

'No.' She could have stamped in frustration. 'I mean—what went wrong? What did I do—or say?'

'Nothing at all.' Again that smile that didn't reach his eyes. 'You were perfect company, my dear. But all good things must come to an end.'

'Is that all you've got to say?'

'No,' he said, with a touch of weariness. 'But this is neither the time nor the place for any deep, meaningful discussions. Go back to your own room, Lydie. We'll talk some other time.'

'When?' she demanded raggedly. 'In another five bloody years?'

'Oh, I think I can promise you an earlier appointment than that.' His voice slowed to a drawl. 'I'm older and wiser now, Lydie. I've no intention of allowing myself to be—displaced again.' He paused. 'Now go back to your own room. Get some sleep, and let me do the same.'

She stared at him, her eyes transfixed by the grace of his lean body, and was dismayed by the uncompromising harshness of his expression.

She said, her voice breaking, 'Marius, don't treat me like this—I can't bear it.'

'What the hell have you ever had to bear—in the whole of your spoiled, manipulative life?' The savagery in his voice cut her to the bone. 'You weren't the exile, cut off from everything you care about.' Two long, swift strides and he was beside her, his hands gripping her shoulders, bruising her skin. 'Well—were you?'

She gasped. 'You're hurting me.'

He said between his teeth, 'Not as much as I'd like to,' and almost flung her from him. 'Now will you get out?'

'No,' she almost shouted back at him. 'I want an answer—a real answer.'

His mouth twisted. 'Do you, my beautiful one, my madonna lily?' He came to her side. 'Then you shall have one.' He pushed her robe from her shoulder, sliding down the strap of her nightgown to follow it. He bent, letting his mouth slowly graze her bare shoulder, his fingers cup her breast. He said thickly, against her skin, 'Does that tell you what you want to know?'

She shook her head, sudden tears blinding her as she pulled away from him. She turned towards the door, but as she reached for the handle Marius stopped her, pulling her round to face him again.

His face looked bleak suddenly, almost haunted. He said unevenly, 'Oh, God, Lydie—this is the last thing...' She heard his breath rasp in his throat. 'What are you doing to me...?'

His mouth found hers with raw, passionate urgency, his hand tangling in her tumbled hair, pulling her head back so that his lips could travel down the sweet, vulnerable line of her throat.

Her own breath caught in a kind of shaking delight. She let her hands slide up over the damp, hair-roughened skin of his chest to his shoulders and cling there as he kissed her feverishly, his lips lingering in the hollows of her neck and shoulders.

He lifted her and carried her over to the bed, his hands shaking as he pulled apart the edges of her robe, staring down at her, the grey eyes no longer cool but hot and clouded with desire. Time stopped—rolled back. She was a young girl again, desperate with love, on fire for the man touching her body with such trembling, aching reverence.

'You're so beautiful,' he'd whispered to her then. 'All cream and gold, like some exquisite madonna lily. I'm half-afraid to touch you.'

She felt her body slacken, moisten in longing, remembering how she'd reached up, drawn him down to her, mouth warm, hands eager.

'Don't be afraid,' she'd pleaded huskily. 'I'm not. I—I love you...'

And Marius had bent, kissing the words into silence on her lips, feeding her hunger with his as his mouth moved slowly down her body, caressing her breasts, teasing the tender nipples, exploring the curves and hollows of her belly and hips, until he'd found the soft gold calyx of her womanhood.

When at last he'd entered her, she'd cried out, less in pain than surprise and joy at the completeness of it.

She'd been too dazed with pleasure and need to realise then, as she had later in the bruised and bitter aftermath of his departure, that he'd spoken no words of love or commitment in return.

But she remembered now, even as she shivered with delight as his mouth suckled at her breast, flicking her nipple with his tongue. Even as her body arched against his exploring hand in mute self-offering.

She thought, it doesn't matter. If this is all, then I'll take it anyway. Oh, God, it's been such a long time...

She watched him lift himself above her, saw the flare of colour along the strong cheekbones, the faint pearling of sweat on his shoulders and forearms. She was more than ready for him, her body a moist, warm pool in which they both could drown.

Then, with shocking suddenness, he flung himself away from her, throwing himself back on the adjoining pillow, chest heaving, muscles in his throat working almost convulsively as he sought to regulate his breathing.

'Marius?' Lydie raised herself onto one elbow. Her hand moved to stroke back his hair, wipe the beading of sweat from his forehead.

His fingers snapped round her wrist like a manacle, preventing her.

He said hoarsely, almost menacingly, 'Oh, no, Lydie. Not this time, sweetheart. I won't be caught in your honey-trap again.'

Bereft, confused, she stared down at him. 'I don't understand.' She had to force the words past the tightness in her throat. 'Don't you—want me?'

His brief laugh was harsh, unamused. 'God, yes. You know—none better—just how desirable you are. But this time I'm making the rules. And this isn't going to happen.'

He swung himself off the bed, adjusting the loosened towel, then paused suddenly, turning towards the door, his eyes narrowing, his face grimly intent.

'Well, what do you know?' he said half to himself as a knock sounded at the door. 'I think I've been ambushed.'

Lydie scrambled to the floor, dragging up the bodice of her nightgown to cover her bared breasts. Her hands shook as she pulled her robe around her.

She said, her voice cracking a little, 'What is it? Who's there?' and Marius flung her a look of derisive impatience.

'Don't play the innocent,' he advised harshly. He walked to the door and flung it wide.

'What's the matter, Aunt Debra?' His tone was light but challenging. 'The old insomnia playing up again?'

Debra Benedict stood in the doorway, wrapped in her dragon kimono. Her face was set, mouth rigid, eyes enormous. She saw Lydie and her expression changed to one of disbelief, and of anger which swept the room like an icy wind.

She took a step forward, a hand flying to her breast in instinctive theatricality.

'Are you both mad?' Her voice vibrated dramatically. 'Oh, God, Marius, how could you do this—after everything that's happened? Haven't you learned your lesson yet?'

Marius looked at her, his mouth curling. 'You would think so,' he agreed drily. 'Underestimating one's opponents is always dangerous.'

There was a heavy step in the passage, and Austin Benedict appeared, head down, eyes darting suspiciously round.

Like a bull coming into the arena, Lydie thought shakily, still fumbling with the sash of her robe: angry—and unpredictable.

He saw Lydie and stopped dead, looking past her to the rumpled bed. The florid colour in his face deepened to crimson.

'What's going on here?' he demanded, his voice an ominous growl.

'Austin, darling.' Debra put a hand on his arm. 'I'm so sorry—I never dreamed...' She paused. 'I needed to talk to Lydie but she wasn't in her room. And then I heard voices—in here.' She gestured prettily, helplessly. 'I—I thought you were asleep. I'd have done anything to spare you the knowledge of this.'

'I don't need sparing.' He shrugged her hand away almost impatiently. His eyes were fixed implacably on Marius. 'But I'll have an explanation.'

Lydie moved. 'Austin—'

He held up a silencing hand. He didn't even glance at her. 'Your mother will deal with you, my girl.' His voice hardened. 'But I'm disappointed in you, lad. It seems I was right about you all along.'

'On the contrary.' Marius's voice, cool, self-possessed, seemed to cut across the almost visible tensions in the room. 'You just arrived a couple of minutes too soon, that's all.'

'What's that?' Austin glared at him. 'You dare to tell me—?'

'Something I hope will please you.' Marius walked to Lydie's side. His hand closed round her icy fingers. His mouth was smiling faintly but his eyes were as deep and cold as a winter ocean. 'Before we were so rudely interrupted, I was just about to ask Lydie to marry me.' He lifted her hand to his lips. The light kiss seared her skin. 'I'm sorry it's another public proposal, darling,' he added softly. 'I hope it won't prejudice my chances.'

There was a tingling silence. Then, 'Well, well,' Austin said slowly. The heat was dying from his face and voice, to be replaced by surprise and pleasure. 'So that's it.'

'Nonsense!' Debra snapped. 'Lydie's already engaged—to Hugh Wingate. It'll be announced just as soon as she comes to her senses.'

'I wouldn't put money on it,' Austin returned genially. 'I'd say Lydie's come to a very different decision. Haven't you, lass?'

It was difficult to breathe. The room was closing in on her. She was aware of them all watching her—waiting. Austin, with that almost tangible air of relief, Debra, white-faced and rigid with anger. And Marius, his expression remote and unreadable. A stranger. Someone she'd never really known. The man to whom she'd given herself, body and soul, only to face the worst kind of rejection. The man who now claimed to want her as his wife, except that there was no warmth or tenderness in his guarded eyes.

She began to tremble inside.

Marius bent until his mouth was almost brushing her ear. He said quietly, 'The door's open if you want to run away again.' His voice sank to a whisper. 'But, unlike Wingate, I shall follow. You belong to me, Lydie.'

It wasn't the declaration she wanted to hear. But if she ran it would have to be away from Greystones—away from Thornshaugh and her existing life. It would be her turn to disappear without word, without trace. And reason and common sense told her to do just that—to go where he would never find her.

Because she couldn't bear to be hurt again. To give her trust and fidelity to a man without faith. She'd have to be crazy to do a thing like that.

'Lydie.' His hands were on her shoulders, turning her to face him. His voice was urgent, almost harsh. 'Marry me?'

And from some echoing distance, light years from sanity, she heard herself say, 'Yes.'

CHAPTER SEVEN

'No!' DEBRA almost shrieked. 'I won't allow it.'

Austin drew her arm through his, patting her hand. 'I think they've both outgrown the stage where they need our permission, love.'

'And don't call me "love".' The snap in her voice came over loud and clear, and Austin's brows drew together in obvious displeasure.

'Now just calm down,' he said with unwonted sharpness. 'This is the best thing that's happened round here for a long time.' His chin jutted aggressively. 'And we don't want any long engagements either. We'll have the banns up straight away.'

Marius's brows lifted sardonically. 'I'm glad you approve,' he said levelly. His eyes went to Debra. 'And I'm sure, in time, you'll agree it's for the best too.'

'Well, of course.' Austin overrode his wife's deathly silence. He gave Marius a brief pat on the shoulder, then swept Lydie into a bear hug. 'Now say your goodnights and let's get some rest. We can start on the details tomorrow.'

He nodded fiercely at them, then put an arm round Debra, who was ashen except for a bright spot of colour burning in either cheek, and led her firmly away.

Suddenly it was very quiet in the room. Lydie felt as if she'd been caught up in some hurricane which had left her bruised and bewildered in alien territory. Marius was staring into space, frowning slightly, apparently lost in his own thoughts. Then he turned abruptly and went into the bathroom, reappearing a moment later, fastening the belt of his towelling robe.

There were only a few yards between them. She watched him, waiting for him to come to her, take her in his arms. But he neither moved nor spoke, and suddenly the distance between them seemed immense, impassable.

His touch still burned on her skin, but Lydie felt as cold as ice.

She thought, There's something wrong here—terribly wrong.

Swallowing past the constriction in her throat, she said, 'Would you mind telling me what all that was about, please?'

'It's perfectly simple.' His tone was clipped. 'You and I are now engaged to be married.'

'So it seems,' she said quietly. 'But why?'

'Self-preservation, pure and simple.' He threw her a derisive look. 'As you must know.'

'What do you mean?' Her confusion deepened.

He shrugged. 'Austin is one of the last major Puritans. If you'd cried rape, I'd have been out on my ear for good this time. Instead, thanks to your unexpected but gratifying co-operation, we have Austin's blessing. End of story.'

'But nothing happened.' Her voice shook.

'Indeed it didn't,' Marius agreed levelly. 'In spite of overwhelming temptation. But I've been convicted on circumstantial evidence before and that makes me—wary. I can't allow myself to be set up again, Lydie. I have far too much to lose this time around.'

He paused, the grey eyes sweeping her in sensual, insolent appraisal. 'Although I've lost out in other ways, of course,' he added lightly. 'Your body's even more entrancing now than it was when you were seventeen, if that's possible. You've ripened, Lydie, like some exquisite wine.' His smile was tight-lipped. 'What a pity I won't be able to savour every last drop of you.'

She said hoarsely, 'What are you talking about? I don't understand this—any of it.'

'Well, don't let it worry you, Madonna Lily,' he drawled. 'You helped defuse a tricky situation, admittedly of your own making, and I'm grateful. It seems you've developed a conscience along the way.'

He paused. 'And don't be afraid that I'll hold you to your promise. Our engagement is merely an emergency measure—purely temporary, I assure you.'

'Temporary?' Lydie repeated blankly. Her mind was reeling.

'Naturally,' he said. 'I have—other plans.'

An image of Nadine's glowing, sensual beauty seared her mind. The pain of it made her want to cry out, and she sank her teeth into her lower lip.

He was watching her. 'Or did you by some chance think I meant it?' he asked softly.

From a hitherto unguessed-at reserve of courage, Lydie summoned a smile. 'Of course not,' she said, and shrugged. 'Just—glad to have been of service.' She paused. 'But Austin certainly believes you meant it, and that might be a problem.'

'Austin has a strong streak of sentimentality.' He shrugged again. 'And an old-fashioned liking for strings to be tied in neat bows. We'll have to persuade him gradually that this is one knot that would strangle us both.'

She nodded. She wanted to wrap her arms round her body and howl her pain and humiliation, but her voice was cool. 'How long will we need to go on pretending?'

'It's debatable, but I won't allow the charade to drag on unnecessarily.' He gave her a sardonic look. 'You're your mother's daughter, Lydie. Don't tell me play-acting's beyond you.'

'No,' she said. Covered by the skirt of her robe, her hands balled into fists. 'But I prefer to choose my own roles.'

'Don't we all?' His mouth twisted. 'Now, you'd better go back to your own room before Austin comes back and pre-empts us with a shotgun wedding—a performance neither of us would relish.'

He walked to the door and held it open for her. 'Goodnight, Lydie. Sleep well,' he added as she walked away from him down the passage to her own room.

His parting words had been intended as a joke, of course, she thought as she tossed and turned, sheets and covers tangling damply round her restless body, tormented by shame and an aching bewilderment.

She understood little of what had happened—except that she'd offered herself and been refused with a casual cruelty which made her weep inside. That was the stark— the only—reality of the situation.

The rest was an enigma.

She went back over the events of the evening, trying to make sense of them.

Marius, she realised, had deliberately allowed her to think that he'd come back to claim her, that he still wanted her. Earlier in the restaurant he'd been wooing her, as shaken by need, or so she'd have sworn, as she was herself. Yet claiming her had been far from his real intention.

The sobering truth, she told herself forlornly, was that she'd been fooling herself all these years. She'd imagined feelings, attributed emotions which didn't exist. Marius had used her then, and, for his own inexplicable reasons, he was still using her now.

A set-up. The phrase niggled in a corner of her mind, refused to go away. As did 'It seems you've developed a conscience along the way.'

As if he was blaming me, she thought blankly. As if I'd planned for us to be found together.

But the truth was that ever since his return Marius had been manipulating her—all of them—gaining some kind of ascendancy, of which this pseudo-engagement was a part.

And she'd let it happen, she knew sadly, because deep inside she'd still cherished dreams, hopes, childish fantasies of love and happy ever after, with Marius, as he always had been, at the centre of those dreams.

She had never wanted anyone else, and she never would. But that didn't mean he had to feel the same.

A sob rose in her throat and was choked back. Well, she could not and would not endure any more. In the morning she would tell him that the pretence was at an end, make any excuse to Austin that he wanted.

And she would move out, even if it meant sleeping on Nell's sofa, because to share a roof with him after this was unthinkable. Unbearable.

It was a long time before she slept, and when she woke it was late on a clear Sunday morning which lived up to its name in glowing brightness.

The better the day, the better the deed, Lydie thought wearily as she turned on the shower. She felt muzzy and disorientated, and hoped that the water would clear her head. She needed all her wits about her today, and more, she decided grimly, forcing down the raw ache in the centre of her being.

Sunday breakfast at Greystones was always a buffet affair, and Lydie found the dining room empty, apart from Mrs Arnthwaite who was pointedly hovering, waiting to clear away.

Lydie poured herself a cup of coffee and took it into the garden, where she found Jon brooding over the *Sunday Times* crossword.

'Where is everyone this morning?' Lydie tried to sound casual as she took an adjoining chair.

'Mother's in bed, having a migraine.' He didn't look at her. 'Austin and Marius have been at the mill since first thing—another cosy high-level conference.' He smiled bitterly. 'I'm beginning to know how a turkey must feel when it hears carol singers.'

'They didn't ask you to attend?' Lydie bit her lip. 'Oh, Jon.'

'Oh, I was invited to accompany them all right,' he said with a shrug. 'But only to bring your car back. Our new managing director was being managing,' he added tautly.

He tossed the paper down beside his chair. 'I understand congratulations are in order. And also why you slid out of that embarrassing little confrontation last night. I'm not surprised Ma's got a headache. I thought she was going to explode when you didn't show.'

'Confrontation?' Lydie echoed, then realised he meant the dinner party with Hugh. She grimaced. 'I slid out of nothing, believe me.'

'Oh, I don't know. Getting engaged to the future master of all he surveys seems like a sound move.'

Lydie winced inwardly. She needed to talk, but Jon in his present mood was the last person in whom she could confide.

'You look like hell,' she remarked candidly. 'Heavy night?'

'And an even weightier day in prospect,' he said morosely.

'It may not be that bad.' She wished with all her heart that she could believe it. Everything seemed to be slipping away, out of control for all of them.

'It already is.' His smile had a bitter edge. 'Marius has all the evidence he needs. The last few months have been disastrous—botched orders, cancellations, undercutting by other mills. One whole fabric run wasted because we got the colour wrong. Two of our best customers telling me we're unreliable and they're looking elsewhere. It's been a nightmare.'

'But you're not solely to blame, surely?'

'I'm sales director,' he returned. 'The buck stops with me.' He looked much younger suddenly, and frightened. 'And a lot of the mistakes were mine, Lydie.'

'Then why not take matters into your own hands?' Lydie leaned forward, trying to speak robustly. 'You're an artist, love, not a salesman. Ask Marius to transfer you to the design department—or, better still, get out of Benco altogether. Get some formal art training and build a whole new life. Nell will back you every inch of the way.'

'You make it sound all so bloody simple,' he said wearily. 'But it isn't. I can't afford to finish with Benco. Lose that and I'll lose everything else, Nell included.'

'I think you're doing her an injustice,' Lydie said gently. 'Look, why don't we go off somewhere—take some food and drive up onto the moors? We can talk it all through, and you can paint. It's been ages since you did that.'

He shook his head. 'Not today, sis. I've got some serious thinking to do.'

Lydie could only hope it wasn't through the bottom of a glass again. She sighed. 'Well, I think I'll go anyway. I need to blow some cobwebs away, do some thinking of my own.'

His mouth twisted. 'I thought all your decisions had been made?'

'No,' she said, with painful lightness. 'Not necessarily.'

She went up to her room to fetch her bag and a jacket. No matter how hot the day, there was always a breeze on the tops, and she genuinely needed to be on her own and breathe some fresh moorland air. Greystones suddenly seemed oppressive, its atmosphere weighed down with past mysteries and future uncertainties.

As she emerged onto the landing, she saw Mrs Arnthwaite coming out of her mother's room with a grim expression and an untouched breakfast tray.

Lydie hesitated. Experience had taught her long ago that Debra's migraine attacks existed mainly in her own imagination. On the other hand, her mother had been genuinely thrown by last night's events.

If the engagement was such anathema to her that it had made her take to her bed, then perhaps Lydie should reassure her—put things straight.

I certainly owe it to Austin, she told herself with reluctant humour. He has to bear the brunt of mother's attacks, after all.

She tapped quietly on the door and went in. The room was in semi-darkness, and frowsty with stale perfume and used air.

Lydie grimaced and went to the window, pulling back the curtains and opening one of the casements. When she turned back to contemplate the wide bed with its frilled peach draperies, a feeling of shock went through her.

This was no play-acting, she thought, viewing Debra's ravaged face and hollow eyes. Her mother was really ill.

'Darling.' She sat on the edge of the bed and took one of the slim, shaking hands in hers. 'What is it? Do you want me to get a doctor?'

Debra moved her head in almost convulsive negation.

'Then what's wrong? Is it Marius?' The sudden tension, strong as an electric current, which jolted her mother's body gave her the answer she needed.

She said soothingly, 'You mustn't do this to yourself. There's nothing to worry about. I promise you, I'm not going to marry him...'

Debra reared up on her pillows. She said hoarsely, 'What do you mean? What are you talking about? You have to marry him—you must...'

Lydie stared at her. 'But last night you were appalled at the very idea. And, anyway, the engagement isn't a real one. He's just playing some kind of game.'

Debra's fingers closed round hers with painful sharpness. 'Then you've got to play it too. Go along with anything he wants. Accept anything he says or he'll destroy me—all of us.'

'I think,' Lydie said, trying to be patient, 'that you're overdramatising again.'

Debra's laugh was harsh, torn from her throat. 'You think so? Lydie, I tell you he's come back for one thing—for his revenge.'

'But that's crazy.'

Debra shook her head. 'He blames us—me—for having him sent away.' She began to cry. 'I knew about the girl—the pregnancy. I told Austin. I told him...'

Lydie felt sick at heart. 'Don't you think Austin would have found out anyway?'

'I don't know.' Her mother's voice was choked by sobs. 'But it doesn't matter, because I told him and Marius knows. He knows, and he hates me for it. And now he's going to do the same to me. He's going to have me sent away...'

'He can't. He wouldn't.' Lydie felt helpless under the onslaught of such violent emotions. 'Not for telling the truth.'

Debra shook her head, rocking backwards and forwards. 'You don't know,' she said. 'You don't understand.'

Lydie watched her with misgiving. There was something terribly wrong here—far more than her mother was admitting.

She said carefully, feeling her way, 'Mother—is there something you haven't told me?'

'I don't know what you mean.' Debra was defensive. 'I did what I had to do.' She stared past Lydie. 'I never thought he'd come back,' she said, half to herself. 'Austin was so angry—so terribly angry.' She beat at the pillow with her clenched fist. 'I counted on him never coming back.'

'And now he's here,' Lydie said quietly.

Debra clutched at her hand. 'Lydie, you've got to help me. Do whatever he says. Play along with whatever he wants. Don't let him destroy me—my marriage.'

'Is that why you turned up in his room last night? To plead with him?'

Debra moved restlessly. 'Perhaps. I don't know. I wasn't thinking straight. But he'd listen to you. You could make him listen. He wants you, Lydie. He always has...'

'Not any more,' Lydie said wearily. 'I told you—the engagement's a fake.'

'But you could make it real,' Debra urged. 'A clever woman can make a man do anything—'

'No.' Lydie detached herself from the clinging hands and stood up, feeling slightly sick. She said quietly, 'I'll talk to him, certainly. I have to for my own sake. But I can't promise more than that.'

She went to the door, ignoring the tremulous 'Lydie' which pursued her.

She went down to her car, but she made no attempt to start the engine. She was trembling, her stomach churning, her mind running in all directions.

She felt as if she was stumbling through a maze where, try as she might, she could never find the centre, the answer to the riddle.

By reavealing Marius's secret liaison Debra had undoubtedly behaved spitefully. But her actions were hardly grounds for vengeance. Marius, after all, had been guilty as charged, she acknowledged with a pang. Yet, clearly, her mother was badly and genuinely frightened.

And perhaps, Lydie thought, remembering with what ease Marius had turned the tables the previous night, the callous way he'd destroyed her own pathetic illusions, she had reason to be.

I've got to think, she told herself; to plan how to approach him. Somehow I have to convince him that there's nothing to be gained by punishing Mother.

With a sigh, she drove off. She had no clear destination planned, yet when she found herself on the single-track road leading to High Cragg she realised that it was the only route she could have taken.

It had always been a special place for her. Or it had been once, she amended painfully. It had been the first of the moor's wild places that Marius had shown her, and one which they'd come back to over and over again.

That first time, she remembered, she'd just read *Wuthering Heights* and had secretly imagined herself as Catherine Earnshaw revelling in her forbidden passion for a Heathcliff who bore an astonishing resemblance to Marius.

How sweet and silly, and how innocent it had all been, she thought sadly. But then, she had been innocent, the

darker realities of passion—she would not call it love—
still a closed book to her.

Since then she had tormented herself with images of
all the others Marius could have brought to that high
and lonely spot, reminding herself pitilessly that it could
even be the place where his child had been conceived.

She herself had never gone back. Until now, when
invisible threads seemed to be drawing her there.

Today the moor was a smiling place, its rolling, rock-
scarred landscape studded with clumps of gorse like
golden flame and the occasional stubborn tree bending
its back to the prevailing wind. Sheep nibbled sleepily
on the close green turf, while above them a hawk circled
slowly and purposefully, scanning the terrain below for
tell-tale scurryings.

Lydie parked off the road, in a shallow gully dug out
by the Ice Age thousands of years before, and set off
across the uneven rising ground to where the group of
huge, lichen-encrusted boulders reared like a beacon on
the skyline.

In spite of the recent dry spell, the ground was still
boggy in places, and she moved carefully, ruefully aware
of the inadequacy of her flimsy leather sandals.

She was breaking all the rules, but in a world where
chaos suddenly reigned that hardly seemed to matter any
more.

Before she'd covered half the distance she was panting.
Out of condition, she castigated herself mentally. Since
the gallery had started she'd let her aerobics class slide,
and her visits to the local tennis and squash club had
become infrequent.

Leaving Greystones would only be part of the turning
point in her new life, she told herself with determination. It was time to let go of the past and its pain and
concentrate all her energy on the future.

She broke into a run, pushing herself up the steepening slope until she reached the rocks, sagging gratefully against the support of the nearest as she recovered her breath.

The view was amazing—stark but splendid for mile after windswept mile, as far as the eye could see. In another month the heather would be in bloom, covering each undulation in a carpet of pink, crimson and purple.

The stone behind her felt pleasantly warm as she leaned against it, but Lydie wasn't fooled. On the horizon clouds were moving, massing, and the breeze had freshened, striking a chill through her thin shirt. Everything signalled a capricious change to the pleasant day.

Her visit would only be a fleeting one after all, she thought with a sigh, so she would have to take full advantage of the peace and solitude it offered.

Here she could think—without pressure, and without distractions.

Then, from the hanging rock beside her, came a scraping sound and a rattle of loose stone. A shadow descended, landing beside her as lithe and silent as a cat.

Lydie recoiled with a cry, bumping her shoulder clumsily against the rock.

He said softly, mockingly, 'So here you are at last, Madonna Lily. And this time we won't be interrupted.'

CHAPTER EIGHT

LYDIE found her voice. 'What are you doing here?'

'Waiting for you.'

'But you didn't know I'd be here.'

Marius's mouth twisted. 'Didn't I?'

The question seemed to burn into the brief, tense silence which enfolded them.

She thought, Of course he knew—just like he's always known. Both of us drawn here—even against our wills— by each other...

She rallied herself. She said crisply, 'I thought you were at the mill—with Austin.'

He shrugged. 'We finished going through the sales reports earlier than expected.' There was a flatness in his tone which confirmed the trouble that Jon had foreseen. 'I dropped him at the golf club and came to find you.'

'Why?'

'Because by now you've had time to think, and you'll want to talk,' he returned laconically. He paused. 'I guessed it would be a conversation best enjoyed in total privacy.'

Her heart missed a beat. She said, 'I didn't see your car.'

'I came by the other road.'

It was, of course, the obvious explanation, but the thought that he'd been able to predict her actions, and had been lying in wait for her here, was still a disturbing one.

She moved abruptly, and winced as the shoulder she'd knocked throbbed in protest.

He noticed instantly. 'What have you done?'

'It's nothing.'

'Really?' he asked sardonically. He put his hands on her arms and turned her so that he could inspect the damage. His touch was gentle but unequivocally insistent. Lydie knew that she could not have pulled away if she'd tried.

Marius was frowning, tight-lipped. 'You've torn your shirt,' he commented. For a heart-stopping moment she felt the brush of his fingers as he lifted the ripped material away from her skin. 'And you're going to have the mother and father of a bruise. Maybe you should have it looked at.'

'And maybe I shouldn't,' she said curtly, stepping back as he released her, hating the way her pulses were pounding. 'I bruise easily.'

'I wouldn't have said so.' There was a note in his voice which grated along her senses. His smile was swift and humourless, his eyes without warmth as he studied her. 'You certainly never used to startle so easily.'

'Perhaps,' she said steadily. 'I used to have less reason to be nervous.'

He nodded meditatively. 'Your thinking seems to have been to good purpose, Madonna Lily.'

Perhaps it was the new edge to the breeze which made her shiver. She looked up at the great mass of cloud advancing steadily towards them.

She thought, 'The bright day is done, and we are for the dark.'

She said slowly, 'I asked you—that first night—why you'd come back. And you didn't answer. I'm asking again now.'

'I came,' he said, 'to reclaim everything that belongs to me.'

'Not for—revenge?' She could hardly believe she'd said the word. Nothing seemed real any more—not the ache of her bruised shoulder, not the ground beneath her feet, or the cool wind bringing the first hint of rain. And certainly not this stranger confronting her across some unthinkable, unbridgeable gulf.

'Ah—revenge.' His mouth twisted. 'A dish best eaten cold—isn't that what they say?'

'I don't know.'

'But you have a horrible suspicion you're going to find out.' His brows lifted mockingly.

She wanted to tell him to do his worst—to go to hell. That she wanted no part of whatever devious, twisted game he was playing with them all. That he'd caused her, surely, enough pain, enough bewilderment for one lifetime. But an image of Debra's frightened, ravaged face rose in her mind and held her back.

She thought, I promised her I'd try...

She lifted her chin. 'I could ask you to be merciful.'

'You'd do better,' he said quietly, 'to ask the price of my silence.'

'I don't think I understand.'

'On the contrary, Madonna Lily.' He spoke with jeering emphasis. 'You understand perfectly well.'

He threw back his head, his eyes as remote and hard as the stones which surrounded them.

He said, half to himself, 'I suppose, at first, I didn't want to believe it—that all that innocence and grace could be turned against me. When Austin sent for me that day, I had no idea what to expect. And, even when I saw he was angrier than I'd ever known him in my entire life, I still didn't realise that I was directly concerned in that anger.

'We'd had our disagreements before, but this was totally different. He was calling me things—using filthy words which I knew were completely alien to him. Shouting at me that I'd betrayed his trust, defiled his home. At times he was almost incoherent.'

Marius shook his head. 'I felt as if I was living through some nightmare—that the world had dissolved into some Kafkaesque vision of insanity.'

He paused. 'And then I saw the letter.'

'Letter?' Lydie felt stunned, her head reeling as she tried to make sense of what he was saying. Austin was a Puritan in many ways, she thought, but he was also a man of the world. Could the news that his nephew had seduced a local girl and made her pregnant really have driven him into such a mad rage? 'What letter?'

'The one I wrote to you.' His voice was almost matter-of-fact. 'Composed in the delirious aftermath of the night we'd spent together and intended, obviously, for no one's eyes but yours. A letter from a man passionately in love to the object of his desire. And, with it, your own note.' He quoted from memory, '"Mother, I think Austin should deal with this."'

'No.' The denial was torn from her throat. 'It's not true—any of it ...'

'Don't bother to lie,' he flung back at her. 'Do you think I don't know your writing? And then, of course, it all came out—how I'd been making sexual advances to you for years, abusing you, destroying your childhood. How you'd stood it as long as you could, but then had found the courage to speak out because you'd discovered, to your horror, that you weren't the only one—and that the other poor little bitch was now pregnant.'

His voice was raw, savage. 'God, Lydie, you're the real actress in the family—lying in my arms, pretending to make plans for us both, to share my life, when all the time you were conniving to be rid of me, to hand the mill—my inheritance—everything I'd worked for—even my uncle's love, for God's sake—on a platter to your brother Jon. And I fell for it. Signed my own death warrant by writing to you. That letter must have been like manna from heaven. You could twist it in any way you wanted. And, by heaven, you did.'

Lydie stood, numb with horror, as his words lashed her quivering senses.

This, then, was it, she thought, the answer to the enigma, the unspeakable secret at the centre of the maze. Like turning over a stone and finding unnamed horrors clinging to the hidden surface.

She felt nausea, acrid and bitter, rise in her throat, and fought it down.

She wanted to scream her denials at him—convince him that his letter—the passionate confirmation of everything they had shared in that sweet and secret night—had never reached her, had been intercepted somehow.

Only she couldn't. Because she knew who was responsible—and why. And only an hour or so previously she had promised to protect her.

Now she could see only too well the reason for Debra's terror, for her insistence that Marius had the power to destroy her.

She thought, But he doesn't blame her—not yet. He blames me. And I'll bear that somehow. I'll have to. Because I can't tell him what really happened. Not now. Not ever.

Because if the whole truth ever comes out it will end the marriage—finish her for ever. And—dear God—it could be the death of Austin too—if he finds out what she's really capable of. Last time, it was touch-and-go. His heart couldn't stand it.

Lydie was falling apart, but in the centre of her mind was a core of ice, telling her what she must do.

The love she and Marius had shared was gone for ever, trampled to death by her mother's obsessive ambition for her son and Marius's own callous betrayal. Whatever pitiful, pathetic hopes she might still have harboured of retrieving some of their past joy in each other, they had ended quite irrevocably. She knew that now. Marius had come back for vengeance, and nothing else.

And the fact that, in spite of everything he had done, she still loved him meant nothing. She had tried so hard to shut him out of her heart and mind in the past lonely years, only to be faced with the realisation that all her efforts had been meaningless.

It was as if she'd been existing in some kind of bleak vacuum, waiting for him to return. But now he was here, and she had to recognise that her long, painful vigil had been in vain.

Well, she thought, her spine straightening almost unconsciously, she could not save her love, but she could, perhaps, provide some salvation for Debra, little though she deserved it. Disgust twisted inside her at the contemplation of her mother's machinations.

But Austin was a different matter. For his sake, if nothing else, she had to try.

If she had lost Marius for ever, what he thought of her no longer mattered. Nothing, she thought detachedly, mattered. Not any more.

So she would accept the guilt and act as scapegoat. Do anything she had to which would prevent him re-examining what had happened and, perhaps, asking questions which could only lead to disaster.

And maybe out of the evil some good might eventually come. Perhaps something could be salvaged from the wreckage of her precious, hopeless dreams.

'Have you nothing to say?' His face and voice were grim.

Lydie shrugged, as if in defiance. 'You seem to have covered the subject pretty thoroughly.' She kept her voice cool.

'And last night? I presume you were attempting to set me up with Austin all over again.'

Her heart thudded. 'Naturally,' she returned.

'So, why did you pull out at the last minute?'

She shrugged again. 'I got cold feet. Maybe I was afraid he might not be quite so gullible the second time around.'

'A quality,' he said gently, 'that he and I share.'

The first gust of rain touched her face like icy needles and she winced. 'Well, there won't be any more attempts,' she said, dredging up a note of insouciance. 'And you don't have to plot to get rid of me. I'll make arrangements to leave Greystones as soon as possible.'

'I'm afraid not.' His clipped tone was as cold as the rain.

'What do you mean?' She was glad of the sudden chill, the squall sweeping towards them. She could pretend that she was trembling from the cold.

'You don't escape as easily as that, Madonna Lily.' His contempt cut into her. 'Going into exile's an easy option compared to what I've got planned for you.'

Lydie stiffened. She said, 'I hope you don't intend me to continue with this farcical engagement you invented.'

'Oh, no. I've decided to dispense with that.' His smile was tight-lipped, the grey eyes glacial. 'Instead, I'm going along with Austin's suggestion and putting the banns up straight away.' He acknowledged her small gasp of shock with a grim nod. 'Although we'll make it a register-office wedding,' he went on. 'The idea of exchanging sacred vows in church with you, my treacherous angel, is a little too much to stomach.'

'You don't mean it,' Lydie said desperately. 'You can't mean it. Not after all you've said...'

'Why not?' His tone was flatly and utterly cynical. 'As far as Austin's concerned, it will wipe the slate clean, remove any lingering doubts he may have about my probity. And as for you...' He paused. 'Well, for you, Madonna Lily, it will be the price of the silence I mentioned to you. I'll keep quiet about the Hatton plot to remove me in return for your public respect and your private—compliance.'

His voice slowed to a drawl. 'Physically, my sweet, you're still everything a man could want. It was too much to hope that you'd have a soul to match. So—I'll take what I can get. At least, unlike most bridegrooms, I won't be starting off with any illusions.

'And neither, my beautiful one, should you. By marrying you, Lydie, I keep you chained safely to my wrist, where I can keep an eye on you. If you and your family wish to hang onto your lifestyle, then that will depend very much on your good behaviour from now on.'

The damp rock under her fingers seemed the only reality in a world gone crazy.

'You seem,' she said thickly, 'very sure I'll agree to this—monstrous bargain.'

'And you,' he said, 'seem to think you have a choice.'

'I could always tell you to go to hell—do your worst,' she flung at him. 'Your own record in all this is hardly unblemished.'

It was raining harder now, the droplets slanting at them on the rising wind. But Lydie was almost oblivious to the changing conditions, her whole concentration fixed tautly on the man confronting her.

His smile was unamused. 'Compared with you, darling, I'm a plaster saint. And my worst could have a devastating effect on all the Hattons. Don't forget that.'

'You're threatening me—my family...'

'At least I'm making my intentions clear, and to your face,' he returned harshly. 'Your brother, for instance. He's totally blown his job as sales director. He can either be moved sideways where he can do less harm or he can become another jobless statistic. That,' he added silkily, 'is entirely up to you.'

He paused. 'And then there's your little hobby at the gallery. If I called in the loan, could you pay it?' His mouth twisted as he saw her stricken expression. 'I thought not.'

She said unevenly, 'But you wouldn't just be hurting me. There's Nell...'

'I'm aware of that.' His tone was clipped. 'But every war has its casualties.' There was a tense silence, then he went on briskly, 'I'm sure I don't have to list some of the other options open to me that you'd find equally unpalatable.'

She knew, without being told, that he meant Debra, and shook her head mutely.

He said sardonically, 'I thought not. Then the bottom line is this, Lydie. You can fight me, and lose. Or you can surrender—on my terms.'

'Marius,' she whispered, 'don't do this—please...'

'Begging?' he asked mockingly. 'It's a bit late for that. Just remember, sweetheart, that only a few years ago I'd have given you everything, including my heart and soul as your toy. But you didn't want that. You preferred to make a grab for the jackpot all by yourself. So be it.' He shrugged. 'This time around the offer is different. And I strongly advise you to save yourself a lot of grief and accept.'

'How,' she said, 'could I possibly save myself from grief in the kind of relationship you're suggesting?'

'By fixing your mind firmly on the alternatives,' he said. 'Anyway, it's hardly a big deal, Lydie. Women sell themselves for far less every day.'

He looked up at the sky and grimaced. 'And now we'd better get under some shelter. I don't want you to die of pneumonia before the deal goes through.'

Before she could draw back, he took her hand and plunged off down the slope towards her car. As they ran there was a sudden flash above them, followed by a crack of thunder, and the heavens opened.

Within seconds they were both drenched, running almost blindly through the downpour, their clothes plastered to their bodies.

Lydie found her sandals slipping on the wet turf and cried out in alarm as her feet slid from under her.

With one deft movement, Marius lifted her off the ground, his arm like steel round her waist, clamping her against his hip as he raced towards the car.

'Key,' he commanded breathlessly as they reached the gully where the Corsa waited. She dragged it from the soaking depths of her pocket and threw it to him. Within seconds the door was open and he'd pushed her inside then hurled himself into the seat beside her. He sat back, eyes closed, chest heaving.

He said hoarsely, 'Ye gods.'

The rain was throwing itself at the car windows as if it was trying to batter its way in, drumming on the roof, pouring in rivulets down the windscreen.

Lydie thought, It's like being trapped inside a waterfall.

She was wringing wet. Her pale blue trousers had darkened almost to navy and her shirt was like a second, unpleasantly damp skin. She glanced down at herself, and saw to her embarrassment how the saturated fabric had moulded itself to her breasts, its near transparency revealing the darker aureoles round her nipples, themselves hardened to unexpected prominence by the sudden chill.

She might as well have been naked.

She twisted round to look on the back seat for a sweater—anything with which to cover herself, and saw him staring at her as if mesmerised, his bottom lip caught in his teeth, his eyes fixed on the revealing shirt with a hunger he made no effort to disguise.

The silence between them was suddenly electric. Lydie was unsure whether the pounding she could hear was the thud of the rain against the car's panels or her own frantic heartbeats.

She tried to say something—make a feeble joke about drying out the car's upholstery—anything to lighten the tension between them, to break the enforced intimacy of their rain-washed prison—but Marius reached across, placing a silencing finger on her parted lips before gently tracing their cold, tremulous softness.

A sigh rose and quivered in her throat. She could feel the blood burning thick and hot in her veins, bringing a flush to her skin, as his hand moved, lifting the damp strands of hair away from the nape of her neck before stroking his fingertips down its smooth, vulnerable length.

She shivered, her throat arching in guilty, delicious pleasure at the caress.

His hand circled the base of her neck, sliding under the damp collar of her shirt, his thumb moving rhythmically over her collar-bone, his touch registering the betraying flurry of the tiny pulse that throbbed there.

Without haste, he smoothed along her shoulder, and down, his fingers coming to rest a tantalising inch from the heated, sensitised peak of her breast.

She wanted him to touch her. Wanted him to open her shirt and take first one, then the other naked, engorged bud into his mouth. Wanted to feel the benison of his lips and tongue on her fevered flesh.

She had never, she thought dazedly, ever wanted anything quite so much in the whole of her life. She had never desired anyone so much. Her being—her womanhood seemed to have been created for this one man—this one moment.

He leaned forward and kissed her on the mouth, his cool lips brushing hers in little more than a sensuous whisper of a caress. At the same time his fingertips feathered lightly over her straining nipples, sending frissons of erotic delight and longing shivering through her entire body.

Only it wasn't enough. She craved everything he had to give with all that she had to offer.

With a faint moan, she seized his other hand and pulled it against her body, pressing it to the moist, scalding core of her female being, mutely pleading for whatever release he could provide.

He said quietly, against her mouth, 'I think not.' And sat back in his seat.

She lifted her heavy lids and looked at him; he was remote, suddenly, and distant, a million miles away from her in the cramped confines of the car. She saw his mouth twisting faintly as he met her bewildered gaze.

'I don't—understand.' Her voice sounded dazed, hoarse.

He shrugged. 'I stopped making love in cars during adolescence. Besides—' the half-smile became a sneer '—I want nothing to spoil the magic and beauty of our wedding night, Madonna Lily. I think—under the circumstances—a special licence, don't you?'

'Damn you,' she whispered rawly. 'Damn you to hell.'

'When I go,' he said softly, 'I'll take you with me.'

He rubbed his sleeve over the misted windscreen. 'And the storm seems to be passing,' he added conversationally. 'I'll go and pick up my car.'

All the heat had drained from her and she felt bitterly, achingly cold.

Marius put a hand under her chin and tilted up her face. He drawled, 'Don't look so desolate, darling. At least our unpromising marriage has one plus going for it. And no lie or pretence can change that.'

He kissed her again, briefly, searingly, and was gone.

Huddled behind the steering wheel, she watched his tall figure stride briskly down the road and out of sight.

This, she realised, shaking, was a foretaste of what he intended their relationship to be. Sex without love. Passion without tenderness. A fever—a sickness without a remedy.

This was to be the price of *her* silence.

And it was only the beginning. Ahead of her, in the future, Lydie could see only bleakness, and a loneliness as deep and cold as a winter ocean.

CHAPTER NINE

LYDIE could never remember afterwards how she managed to get back to the house, yet somehow she found its reassuring bulk rearing up in front of her.

Some sixth sense warned her to park in her usual place, as she would do on any normal homecoming, and this she did, although she knew that nothing would or could ever be normal again.

Then she ran indoors, head bent, through the slackening rain, and straight upstairs, making grimly for Debra's room.

All the way home her mind had been in utter turmoil, trying desperately to come to terms with the appalling accusations that Marius had levelled at her, making the kind of connections her spirit shrank from.

Her suspicion that her mother had by no means confessed the whole truth that morning had been proved disastrously correct. In fact, Lydie could hardly believe the depths of deceit which Debra had sunk to.

And for what? she thought, sickened. So that Jon could have Marius's place in the sun. Did she really think she was going to get away with it?

But, of course, she had got away with it—for nearly five years, unchallenged and apparently unassailable until now. Now that Marius, against all the odds, against belief, had returned...

And this is where it ends, she thought, her heart like a stone. She can't expect me to act as scapegoat for her lies, to pay this monstrous price simply to keep her safe.

Mother will have to talk to Marius, she told herself. Persuade him that the truth can only damage Austin—whom we all love. Surely, knowing that, he'll be prepared to make allowances?

She bit her lip. That prospect was uncertain to say the least. Maybe the most Debra could hope for was to throw herself on Marius's mercy.

Whatever, Lydie did not relish having to break the news to her.

But when she reached her mother's room the door was open, and its sole occupant was Mrs Arnthwaite, who was grimly remaking the bed with clean linen.

'Oh.' Lydie checked in the doorway. 'Has Mother recovered from her migraine, then?' she asked constrainedly.

'I reckon she must have.' The housekeeper wrestled a pillow into its case. 'She's gone off to Wheeldon Grange for a day or two. There was a last-minute cancellation, seemingly, so they could take her.'

Lydie's heart sank. Wheeldon Grange was an exclusive up-market health hydro with an emphasis on elegant diets and beauty treatments, a Mecca for the well-heeled and overweight. But the privacy of its guests was rigorously ensured. Lydie had marginally more chance of breaking into Fort Knox than of achieving any kind of confrontation with Debra in the Grange's high-priced and hushed surroundings.

As her mother well knew, she thought bitterly. She'd chosen her sanctuary quite deliberately.

'Do you know when she's coming back?' Her voice sounded hollow. She was ice-cold again, shaking with reaction as she leaned against the doorjamb.

'I couldn't say at all.' Mrs Arnthwaite triumphantly fought the last pillow into submission.

'I see.' Lydie paused, trying to collect her reeling thoughts. 'Is—is my brother at home?'

'Nay, he's gone into Thornshaugh to see his young lady. Told me he wouldn't be back until late.' Mrs Arnthwaite lifted the bedspread into the air like a swirling, silken cloud and lowered it to the bed with symmetrical precision.

Then she turned, her eyes narrowing as she observed Lydie's sagging figure. 'And what's to do here?' She crossed the room with her purposeful stride. Lydie felt her hair, her sleeve touched with an oddly gentle hand, and knew a demeaning urge to throw herself against that ample bosom and sob.

'Why, lass, you're sopping wet—and freezing.' The housekeeper gave a disapproving cluck. 'Now, you come with me, and be quick about it.'

Lydie, too shattered to argue, obeyed.

Before she knew what was happening, she found herself immersed in a steaming, scented bath, with towels and a robe warmed and waiting for her when she emerged. It was wonderful, she thought dazedly, to find someone else in control. Wonderful to have her hair rubbed briskly, then blow-dried quickly and without fuss. Even more wonderful to find the fire lit in her bedroom and a chair set beside it, and then to be presented with a tray bearing a bowl of fragrant, creamy chicken soup, a bread roll still hot from the oven, and a pat of butter in its own cooling dish.

To be pampered like this, and by Mrs Arnthwaite. It was almost beyond belief.

'Mr Austin won't be back from golf until teatime. He's ordered the roast to be served this evening,' the housekeeper explained. 'But this should tide you over.'

'It certainly will.' Lydie forced a smile. 'You've been very kind.'

'And when you've finished your meal you're to have a rest on your bed. You've got the house to yourself, so you won't be disturbed.' She gave Lydie an almost maternal nod. 'And I'll call you in good time for tea.' She paused at the door, her expression almost arch. 'Mr Marius will have returned by then too.'

Well, that explained Mrs Arnthwaite's change of attitude, Lydie thought as the door closed behind the older woman. I'm no longer an interloper in her eyes, but the future mistress of the house. And that makes all the difference.

If she hadn't felt so heartsore, it would have been almost funny. But she was genuinely glad to hear that Jon had sought out Nell at last. Maybe, with his future at the mill in doubt, they could now reach some kind of rapprochement. Certainly her brother needed Nell's steadfast support as never before. If he'd recognised this, it was a step in the right direction at least, she decided with a small sigh as she began to eat. Her own conflicts were a different matter, however.

She still felt battered and emotionally bruised by the events of the morning, but the soup was a delicious comfort and she finished every drop.

Her meal over, she lay back in the chair, watching the small pile of apple logs that Mrs Arnthwaite had kindled in the hearth dwindle and disintegrate into sweet-smelling ash.

Rather like my life, she thought wearily, and felt a slow tear trickle down her cheek.

Suddenly she felt stifled, claustrophobic. She went over to the window, pushing the casement wide and drawing in deep breaths of air. The weather was improving, with a watery sun making a grudging appearance between the scudding clouds. The air was fresh with the recent heavy rain, the clean, sharp scent of grass intermingled with the intoxicating perfume from the massed beds of roses and the languorous, glorious fragrance of the lilies, clustered against the house's rough grey walls.

Lydie tensed as the heady, evocative sweetness reached her, caressing her senses, reawakening memories that were half-pleasure, half-pain. For her, the perfume of the lilies would always mean moonlight spilling across a bed, the warmth of Marius's arms around her, the sensuous caress of his hands and lips against her flesh, arousing her to undreamed-of pleasure.

And only a short while ago, for a few, brief moments, she'd glimpsed that same delight again. Known the same driving, aching need.

Yet it wasn't the same, she realised sadly. It couldn't be. Because all Marius was offering her now was physical passion without any of the underlying tenderness and reverence of love. And that, for her, would never be enough.

She shivered slightly and turned away from the window. Perhaps a sleep would do her good, she thought, climbing onto the bed and pulling the coverlet across her body. At least it would provide her with a period of welcome oblivion from her problems.

But even in sleep there seemed no escape. Her dreams were fleeting and restless. She seemed to move uneasily through alien landscapes, surrounded by the faces of strangers. When she tried to speak, no words came. Everything she touched seemed to dissolve into nothingness. And out of the blankness came mocking voices, taunting her, calling her names.

One of the voices became louder, more persistent. She felt herself being shaken, not roughly, but sufficient to jerk her into wakefulness with a small, frightened cry.

She sat up in dazed alarm, pushing her hair back from her face, and saw Marius standing beside the bed.

He said with cool formality, 'I'm sorry if I startled you. I came to tell you that Austin is back and demanding his tea.' He paused, then added expressionlessly, 'And he's brought a visitor.'

'Oh?' Lydie still felt disoriented. 'Who is it?'

'George Foxton.' Marius allowed her to assimilate the name of Thornshaugh's leading jeweller. He added tonelessly, 'Apparently he ran into him at the golf club and persuaded him to bring over a selection of rings especially for you to choose from.'

'Rings?' Lydie repeated in bewilderment, and Marius nodded with slight impatience.

'Austin clearly wishes to formalise our engagement without delay,' he said, his lips twisting. 'I take it you have no objection?'

'I have at least a thousand objections.' Lydie strove for poise, her eyes challenging him. 'Not that I suppose they make any real difference.'

'You're learning, Madonna Lily.'

Yes, she thought, and in a hard school. Aloud, she said, 'Austin certainly isn't wasting any time.'

Marius hunched an indolent shoulder. 'He probably feels too much time has been wasted already,' he retorted.

'Oh,' she said, and stretched. 'In that case, I'd better get dressed.'

'Perhaps so.' He looked at her for an intent, tingling moment. Lydie, following the direction of his eyes, saw that the lapels of the towelling bathrobe had fallen apart during her restless doze, leaving her almost naked to the waist.

Colour stormed into her face. She said, 'Oh,' again, this time in vexed embarrassment, and covered herself swiftly, aware of his faint smile.

He said, 'Actually, you can take your time. I've warned him I have to shower and change.'

Taking her first good look at him, Lydie was shocked to see that he was still wearing the clothes he'd had on earlier. She said, dismayed, 'You mean you've only just come back? Marius—for God's sake—you'll end up with pneumonia...'

'I'm sorry to depress your hopes,' Marius said dismissively, 'but it will take slightly more than a summer storm to carry me off. However, I appreciate the note of wifely concern,' he added, his mouth slanting sardonically. 'It sounded almost genuine. You must have been rehearsing, sweetheart.' He paused, watching the flare of indignant colour in her face. 'Why not complete the caring picture by coming with me to wash my back?' he invited softly.

For an instant, the image of him tanned and naked under the torrent of hot water invaded her mind with startling clarity. She could almost breathe the damp scent of his skin, feel the depth of bone and play of muscle as she ran her hands across his shoulders, and down the length of his spine...

She said breathlessly, hauling herself back from the edge of some inner precipice, 'I'm afraid my concern doesn't go to those lengths.'

'Ah, well,' he said, and his smile was slow and devastating. 'It's early days. See you later.'

Watching him walk to the door, Lydie was tautly aware that her heart was thudding against her ribcage, and, more frighteningly, of exactly how tempted she was to call him back.

As soon as the door closed behind him, she scrambled off the bed and ran to the wardrobe.

The first garments she grabbed were jeans and a sweatshirt, then, remembering her role as hostess, and in deference to Austin's known preference, she selected a simple shirtwaister dress, narrowly striped in black and white. She brushed her hair back, confining it at the nape of her neck with a black ribbon, and slid her feet into low-heeled pumps. A modicum of make-up would suffice, she thought. A touch of blusher, a trace of highlighting for her eyes, a soft, clear pink to warm the frozen contours of her mouth. Neat but not gaudy.

She stood back and regarded herself, striving for objectivity. Well, she told herself, she was ready—or at least as ready as she would ever be.

As she left her room, Marius joined her on the landing. He was wearing tailored grey trousers and a classic white shirt, the sleeves of which were turned back to reveal his tanned forearms. His dark hair, she saw, was still damp from the shower, and she felt her face warm slightly as she recalled her recent fantasy, thankful that he could not read her thoughts.

She was aware of his eyes travelling over her in a lazy, insolent inspection.

'I like the demure look, Lydie,' he drawled. 'It's almost as beguiling as your recent striptease. Is this a new image?'

'What, this old thing?' she jibed, pinching a fold of fabric between finger and thumb. 'Goodness, Marius, you have been away a long time.'

His eyes narrowed. 'Something of which I need no reminder from you, believe me.' The grim note in his voice sent a chill down her spine. There was something ruthless about him—something implacable. Even if Debra confessed everything and begged his forgiveness, there was no guarantee that it would be granted.

Was he really so set on obtaining his pound of flesh that he would allow the past to destroy them all?

She looked down at the carpet. 'I'm sorry,' she muttered stiltedly. 'It was a stupid thing to say.'

'Unwise, certainly,' he said curtly.

'On the other hand,' she went on bravely, 'neither of us can be expected to take out every word and examine it before we speak.'

He raised his brows. 'What are you suggesting—some kind of truce?'

No, she cried out silently. Not a truce—a lasting peace. And if you were to hold out your arms I would run into them now, and stay there for ever.

She felt her nails score the palms of her hands as she fought for self-control.

She managed a shrug. 'I suppose so.'

'I'm not fond of truces, Madonna Lily,' he said softly. 'I prefer unconditional surrender.'

'And if I find that unacceptable?'

'Austin is waiting for us,' he mused. 'So unfortunately we haven't time now to discuss the range and level of acceptance I require from you. That will be a pleasure to come.' He saw the flinch she could not disguise and smiled faintly. 'Only one of many, of course,' he added silkily. 'Now, shall we go down?' He held out a hand to her.

Lydie ignored it. 'What I will never understand,' she said between her teeth, 'is why Austin ever decided to allow you back into this house at all.'

Marius's smile widened. 'Perhaps, my sweet, he had no choice.' He paused. 'Rather like yourself.'

For a long, measuring moment they looked at each other, then Lydie spun on her heel and walked away from him down the stairs, her head held high.

He caught up with her at the drawing-room door, his hand on her shoulder turning her easily to face him.

'In view of Austin's visitor,' he said softly, 'I think we should burnish our act a little.'

He pulled her towards him and kissed her on the mouth, very slowly, very expertly and very thoroughly, while one hand sought and cupped the soft weight of her breast through the fabric of her dress.

The world seemed to shiver and grow still, encasing them in a heated, thunderous silence.

Lydie's lips parted helplessly under the aching, draining pressure of his kiss. Her senses were overwhelmed by the intimate closeness of his body, the cool, clean scent of his skin, the softly erotic friction of his thumb across her hardening nipple, and, most potent of all, the thrust of his lean, muscular leg between her pliant thighs.

She was oblivious of time, of place, aware only of the clamour of her driven, haunted body pleading for surcease.

When at last he released her, Lydie swayed towards him. Her legs were shaking, the breath labouring in her lungs as she raised dazed and heavy lids and stared up at him. But he seemed, she realised with shock, totally unmoved.

For a moment, he scanned her face with minute attention, then nodded. 'That's better,' he murmured, half to himself. 'At least now you look like a—'

'Please don't say a woman in love,' she threw at him with the scorn of desperation as she dragged together what rags of control she had left, 'or I may throw up.'

His mouth twisted. 'Maybe a woman in lust would be more appropriate,' he drawled. 'Anyway, it's the effect I wanted, and more. Something, darling, you can't pretend—or lie about.'

He reached past her to open the door, then motioned her to precede him into the room with exaggerated courtesy.

Austin and George Foxton were just coming in from the garden.

'So there you are.' Austin was clearly in one of his most genial and expansive moods. 'George has a little surprise for you, my dear.' He nodded towards a flat black case on a side-table. 'That's only a small selection, of course. If there's nothing that appeals, you could always choose a stone and have a ring made for you.'

Lydie was tautly aware of Marius at her shoulder. She said lightly, 'I'm sure there's no need to go to those lengths. Anything will do.'

'Anything?' Austin's brows lifted in surprise and the beginning of displeasure.

'I think Lydie means that she doesn't need diamonds to remind her of our happiness,' Marius interposed smoothly. He smiled down into her eyes, challenging her. 'Think of it, darling, as a symbol of our love for each other.'

She found herself seated at the table, George Foxton making a little ceremony of unlocking the case. His was a long-standing family business, and he had a name for being a shrewd judge of gems.

In spite of her anger and inner tension Lydie gave a faint gasp as he drew away the layer of black velvet and the brilliance of the stones flared into the afternoon sunlight.

She thought, This could have been the happiest moment of my life, and saw the glitter of diamonds fragment and blur as sudden tears gathered and were fiercely fought back.

She said huskily, 'They're beautiful.' Then, to Marius, she added, 'Choose for me.'

She was conscious of the weight of his arm, laid casually across her shoulders, the warmth of his breath fanning her cheek as he bent closer, the dark face absorbed.

He said at last, 'This one, I think,' and picked up a cluster ring, the centre brilliant surrounded by baguette diamonds.

'An excellent choice.' Mr Foxton was smiling, the disruption of his Sunday afternoon clearly secondary to the importance of obliging an old friend, not to mention making such a handsome sale, Lydie thought with sudden cynicism.

She found herself hoping absurdly that the ring wouldn't fit, that some adjustment would have to be made before she needed to wear such an obvious sign of Marius's possession of her. Of her submission to his will.

But it slid smoothly and with a kind of finality over her knuckle. She was aware of Mr Foxton's hearty good wishes, Austin's hug, then Marius quietly, almost formally lifting her hand to his lips. Sealing the deed with a kiss.

She forced a smile. 'I'll ring for tea.'

'Tea be damned,' Austin declared robustly. 'I told Mrs Arnthwaite to put some champagne on ice.'

With Mrs Arnthwaite came more congratulations. Lydie felt her smile turning into a fixed grimace. She drank some of the chilled sparkling wine, trying to infuse a little radiance into her expression, into her thoughts, wishing that she did not feel so cold, so dead inside.

Mr Foxton was all smiles as he took his leave, but Lydie knew that he must be secretly wondering at the speed of the engagement following so closely on Marius's return, plus the fact that Debra was absent from such a significant occasion.

But he would never ask, she thought. Never make any comment. He and Austin were friends from their schooldays, members of the same clubs, fellow

Rotarians—pillars of the Thornshaugh old-boy network and subject to its laws of discretion.

Once they were on their own again, Austin insisted on pouring more champagne.

'This is a day to remember.' He waved aside Lydie's protest as he refilled her glass. 'It's a while since there's been much worth celebrating in this house. A whole new beginning.' He nodded fiercely. 'That's what we all need.'

But how could there be, Lydie asked herself wretchedly, with so much left unsaid? With so many lies and half-truths still hanging over them all? Could it all be simply swept aside and out of sight, as Austin seemed to think?

And, more importantly, could she and Marius build a relationship, or any kind of happiness, on such dangerous foundations?

But Marius didn't want a relationship, she reminded herself desolately. He was taking her in revenge. To punish her for a crime she had not committed.

'We thought a quiet wedding,' Marius was saying, and she forced herself to focus on his words. 'At the register office in Thornshaugh, as soon as they can slot us in.'

Austin looked pugnacious. 'It'll be properly arranged all the same. No hole-and-corner job.'

'Naturally,' Marius agreed. 'But there's far too much to be done at the mill to permit a full dress affair. We'll even have to postpone a proper honeymoon until work eases a little. It's fortunate that Lydie's so understanding.' The smile he sent her did not reach his eyes.

'Well, I can't say I'm sorry,' Austin admitted. 'I've never fancied parading around in that damned monkey suit, and that's the truth.'

'Besides,' Marius added silkily, 'I can't wait for months of wrangling over invitations and vol-au-vents and bridesmaids' dresses to claim my wife. Can I, darling?'

His glance was a challenge, his words a gauntlet flung down between them, daring her to speak, to throw them back in his face.

'No.' Her voice was like a thread. The ring on her hand felt clumsy, alien in its magnificence. It burned like a cold flame.

Like passion, she thought detachedly, without love. The icy fire that would consume her until she was totally destroyed.

Unless she could find some means of escape in the brief time still left to her. A way out which would not bring the world of those she loved crashing down around them.

She thought, her heart like stone, I'll find it somehow. I have to...

CHAPTER TEN

LYDIE's primary instinct was to go to her car and simply drive away, put as many miles as she could between herself and the lies, the betrayals and the inevitable heartbreak.

But common sense told her that it could never be as easy as that to disentangle herself from her life at Thornshaugh.

For one thing, how could she simply walk out on Nell and the gallery? she asked herself in a kind of despair. Or leave Austin without a word? It wasn't possible.

'Well, I've got some letters to write.' Austin was getting to his feet. 'I'm sure you two have plenty to talk about between now and dinner.' He gave them both a ponderous wink and left the room.

Lydie suppressed a gasp of dismay.

She said hurriedly, 'Actually, I have things to do myself, if you'll excuse me.'

'Not so fast, Madonna Lily.' Marius's voice was cool but implacable. 'We do need to get a few things settled.'

'I thought you'd already done that.' Lydie lifted her chin. 'I seem to be a puppet in all this—made to dance to any tune of your choosing.'

'You sound a little bitter, my love,' he said mockingly. 'I hope it isn't the loss of our honeymoon that's irking you. I promise it's only a postponement, not a cancellation.'

'That's the last thing on my mind,' she returned curtly. 'Actually, I'm wondering just how far you're prepared to carry on with this—farce.'

'A strange word,' he said, 'to describe my honourable proposal of marriage—and your acceptance of it.'

'Acceptance?' Lydie's laugh cracked in the middle. 'My coercion into it, you mean.' She rose, restlessly, and went over to the French windows. 'The whole thing's surreal. That ghastly ritual over choosing the ring, Austin's pretending to be pleased—'

'Austin is pleased,' Marius cut in abruptly. 'He's a deeply conventional man. To him, our engagement— our marriage—is a way of wiping the slate clean. Of putting the past firmly behind us, where it belongs.' He added lightly, 'His only error is in assuming my motivation is the same as his.'

She shivered uncontrollably, folding her arms in defence across her body.

'Marius—don't do this—please. End it now.' Her voice broke. 'I beg you.'

'How can I end it, Madonna Lily,' he asked softly, 'when it's only just begun?'

She released the catch on the window and stepped out into the garden.

'Running away, Lydie?' His jibe followed her. 'A pointless exercise, darling, because I should certainly come after you.'

'I need to breathe clean air,' she flung back at him over her shoulder. 'I'm sure you understand. And, as I said, I have things to do.'

It wasn't true, she acknowledged as she walked across the grass. She had no plans of any kind. It was simply that there was no way she could spend the rest of the afternoon in virtual seclusion with Marius.

The situation was altogether too dangerous, and she was too vulnerable to cope with the frank temptation it offered. Or even, she thought, with Marius's own dis-

tinctive brand of sexual teasing—the cat-and-mouse
game he was playing with her feelings—her emotions.

But she mustn't think about that. Must learn to ignore
the insidious voices in her head telling her that, in spite
of everything, to separate herself from him for ever
would tear her apart. Leave her bleeding to death for all
eternity.

That was not what she wanted to hear, she thought
raggedly. Because she could not allow herself to love him.
Could not allow herself to accept the sham relationship
that he was trying to force on her. There had been enough
bitterness—enough ruin already. Somehow she had to
make him see that. Persuade him that there was nothing
to be gained from allowing the old sins of the past to
cast their long shadow over the future.

The breeze struck a chill through her thin dress and
she shivered again, reluctant to return to the house,
before remembering that there was a jacket in her car.

The poor thing looked as if it had been abandoned,
she thought, wrinkling her nose, as she rounded the side
of the house and saw it standing forlornly on the drive.

In different circumstances, she would have driven into
Thornshaugh and poured her heart out to Nell. But if
she and Jon were finally making some sense of their own
tortuous relationship Lydie could not intrude there.

No, the gallery was out of bounds today, she decided.
But thinking about it had jogged her memory about an
almost-forgotten errand she had undertaken to run.

The money for the Corbin watercolours, she thought,
sliding in behind the wheel and checking that the slip of
paper was still in her bag. She could deliver that and
make one person's day at least.

Quarry Row, as its name indicated, had originally been
built to accommodate workers taking stone out of the

nearby hillside. But the quarry company had been closed for some years and she'd thought most of the houses were empty, if not actually falling into disrepair.

It was a lonely spot, anyway, Lydie thought as she parked in the lay-by at the bottom of the track. Few people would choose to live at such a distance from the nearest town or without immediate neighbours. Yet perhaps it suited the artistic temperament, she decided with a mental shrug.

The gate of the end house opened with a creak of rusty hinges. As she walked up the cracked concrete path, Lydie noticed a swing on a metal frame standing in the middle of a sparse patch of lawn, and some children's clothes turning briskly on a rotary dryer in the fresh wind.

She was also aware that the cottage door had opened and a girl was standing watching her approach.

She was of medium height with fair hair cut in an unassuming bob and blue eyes that studied Lydie warily and without welcome. In her jeans and sweatshirt she looked tough, capable and even slightly aggressive.

Lydie halted, trying a smile which was not returned.

'You're—Darrell Corbin?' she asked with a trace of uncertainty. 'Have I come to the right place?'

'That depends what you've come for, Miss Hatton.' The voice was unfriendly, the local accent transmuted by something else.

'Oh.' Lydie was taken aback. 'Then you know who I am, why I'm here?'

'You could say that,' the other girl said curtly.

Lydie was frankly nettled by her reception, but decided to persevere. 'I've got some good news for you.'

'I doubt that,' Darrell Corbin responded brusquely. 'Although I suppose I should have expected a visit. What is it—another pay-off?'

Lydie, feeling in her bag for the cheque, halted in astonishment. This girl might be a brilliant artist but she seemed to have an outsize chip on her shoulder. Either that or she was deranged, she thought, swallowing. She said temperately, 'I wouldn't put it quite like that.'

'Well, I would.' Darrell Corbin took a step forward, her eyes fierce. 'So, go back where you came from, Miss Hatton—' she spat the name out as if it were an obscenity '—and take your dirty money with you. I don't want it and I never did.'

'Dirty money?' Lydie repeated bemusedly. 'What on earth are you talking about? I came here in good faith...'

'Good faith?' The contempt in the other girl's voice was almost searing. 'You wouldn't know the meaning of the word, Miss Hatton. Neither you nor anyone from your family.'

'Now just a minute, please.' Lydie was getting angry now. 'You have no right to make statements like that.'

'Well, that's where we differ, Miss Hatton. I think I have every right—under the circumstances.' Darrell Corbin lifted her chin. 'But, contrary to what you might think, I didn't come back to make trouble. There's been too much of that already. I came because Dad was ill and needed me.' A muscle moved beside her mouth. 'Well, he's gone now, so there's nothing to keep me here. I realise that. And I want nothing more from any of you, and that's final.'

'I think there must be some mistake.' Lydie fought to make sense of the torrent of bitter words.

'There was,' Darrell Corbin said harshly. 'And I made it. But I never wanted the money—any of it. And I'd never have touched a penny if I'd known how it was come by.'

She flung her head back, staring past Lydie. 'It was him that I wanted, more fool me, although I knew from the start that it would never work. That he—didn't feel like that. I was never more than a bit on the side—a lay.'

The words seemed to be torn out of her.

Lydie felt as if she was listening and watching from some great distance, caught in a dream from which she could not wake.

She didn't want to hear any more. She wanted to put her hands over her ears, close her eyes, blot out everything that was happening. Yet, at the same time, she knew that wild horses wouldn't have dragged her from the spot; that she had to know everything.

'All the same,' said Darrell Corbin, 'I didn't have to have his baby. That was my choice. I didn't even want him to know. That was all Dad's doing.' Her voice cracked slightly. 'He wasn't a bad man, you see, just weak. And he could never manage money, especially after Mum died. Every penny went into the pub or the betting shop. And when he found out about the baby he said I'd to be taken care of and he was going to Mr Benedict.'

'Oh, God.' Lydie couldn't even be sure if she'd spoken the words aloud. Suddenly, it was difficult to breathe.

'When he told me what he'd done, I was so ashamed. I felt it was—blood money. And the worst of it was I'd used some—to buy things I needed for the baby.' The look she sent Lydie was filled with scorn. 'But I never touched any more, and I never will. Tell him that. And don't think you can come here and buy me off, Miss Hatton, because I'm not for sale, and I never was. And I'm going soon—back south, so you needn't fear you'll hear from me again. I can manage without handouts from the likes of you.'

A child's voice called, 'Mam,' and a small boy came trotting round the corner of the house, slowing, suddenly shy, when he saw Lydie.

'Come here, love.' Darrell Corbin's voice gentled reassuringly as she pulled the child against her, her face inimical as she registered Lydie's fixed, stunned gaze.

'Looking for a resemblance, Miss Hatton?' she demanded scornfully. 'Well, you won't find one. He takes after me, thank God.'

She stepped back, and the cottage door closed in Lydie's rigid face.

For a moment she stood as if rooted to the spot, incapable of movement, then she was running, stumbling down the incline towards her car. Once inside it, she sat, gripping the wheel, making no attempt to start the engine as she stared through the windscreen.

Just when she'd least expected it, the last piece in the monstrous jigsaw had been completed, and the picture it revealed filled her with sadness and horror.

So that was her rival. That was the girl who'd lived in her thoughts and haunted her sleep all these years. A girl whose only mistake had been to fall in love. A girl who'd been paid to go away and keep her mouth shut about the consequences of that love. A girl still harbouring a deep residue of pain and bitterness.

And who could blame her? Lydie thought as she drew a deep, shuddering breath.

And, following Marius's return to Thornshaugh, like some black sheep to the fold, Darrell Corbin had naturally assumed that she was being bribed to keep her distance once again. And that, of course, Lydie knew who she was and all about her. That she was in on the whole ugly conspiracy.

But I wasn't, she thought wretchedly. And I wish it had stayed that way—that she'd just remained part of my imagination, without a name—or a face. That I'd never set eyes on her—or her child. Marius's son.

She flinched from the unwilling acknowledgement as if a whip had been laid across her senses.

Oh, why did I have to come here—to meet her? she asked herself, wincing. Why couldn't she just have taken the money five years ago and gone for good?

Even as she hated herself for allowing the wish, she realised that it could never have been that simple. That, for Darrell Corbin, it had never been a matter of money at all.

'It was him that I wanted'. The words were seared into her brain. Because, in spite of the other girl's anger and scorn, there'd been an underlying note of desolation too. Marius had left a legacy of passion behind him in the ruins of their brief affair and its aftermath.

She could sense, too, how Darrell Corbin must have suffered from Marius's indifference to herself and his child. How it must have hurt to know that she was being bought off, that she wasn't good enough for the Benedicts.

And her stepfather had provided the money for the pay-off, she realised with a pang of disillusion; had made sure the girl had been hustled away somewhere to avoid open scandal.

Oh, Austin, she thought sorrowfully. Austin, how could you?

She looked bleakly down at the glitter of diamonds on her hand, wondering if Darrell Corbin had guessed their significance and been hurt by it.

We have a great deal in common, she thought as pain ripped through her. We both loved Marius. We love him still. And he never cared about either of us, which is something she's learned to live with. Something I have, in turn, to endure somehow.

Because love alone was not enough, and never could be. It had to go hand in hand with trust and mutual respect for a relationship to work.

And, on those grounds, she and Marius had never had a chance at all.

She drew a deep, quivering breath.

She would have to confront him now. That went without saying. Use his treatment of Darrell Corbin as the lever to free herself from him. Put an end to the intrigue and the cruel games once and for all. Maybe even force him to acknowledge that he had a son, so that some good could come at last from the entire unholy mess.

She's luckier than I am, she told herself, gripping the wheel until her knuckles turned white. Because at least she has his child. Whereas I—I have nothing at all. Not even hope.

She let go of the wheel, lifted her shaking hands to her face, and began to weep.

All the way home she silently rehearsed what she would say. Tried to assemble the words and phrases that would gain her freedom, without betraying her inner agony.

He expected her to act a part, she thought. This time she would have to give the performance of a lifetime.

On the way back to Greystones she stopped at the local service station to fill her petrol tank, as usual, for the working week ahead. Life had to go on with at least a semblance of normality, she thought, until she could make a reasoned decision about where she would go and what she would do.

She went into the ladies' room to wash away the tear stains and hide the strain in her pale face with a faint dusting of blusher and a fresh touch of lipstick. It might only be a façade, she thought, eyeing herself judiciously in the spotted mirror, but it seemed to work. Last of all, she removed Marius's ring from her finger and stowed it safely in the inside pocket of her bag.

I can never wear it again, she thought.

As she returned to her car, a Range Rover swung into the forecourt of the garage and Hugh Wingate jumped out of the driving seat.

Lydie groaned inwardly as he strode towards her, but stood her ground, forcing a smile.

'Hello, Hugh.'

'Lydie.' There was a heated flush along his cheek-bones. 'I'm amazed you have the gall to face me.'

'A chance meeting by the petrol pumps is barely a confrontation,' she returned evenly. 'And we were bound to run into each other sooner or later.'

'You took care to avoid me last night.'

'I'm sorry.' She bit her lip. 'But the invitation wasn't mine.'

'Is that all you have to say? After you led me on—made a complete fool of me?'

She bent her head. 'That was unforgivable, I know,' she said in a low voice. 'But it wasn't intentional, you must believe that.'

'I'm not sure I can believe anything you say.' He glared at her, raising his voice to override the noise of passing traffic. 'Rumour has it that you've decided to opt for the Benedict money instead.'

'Then you shouldn't give too much credence to hearsay,' Lydie said quietly, thanking Providence that she'd had the foresight to take off her ring. 'But, whatever happens, I'm sure in my own heart, Hugh, that I've done you a favour, and you'll see that too, one day. We wouldn't have been happy together.'

'And are you so sure Benedict's the man to make you happy?' His voice stung with bitter sarcasm. 'Or don't you mind if he plays the field as long as he pays the bills?'

Lydie drew a sharp breath. She said evenly, 'I think you misjudge us both. And anyway, the question doesn't arise.'

'No? I called in at the Three Horseshoes for a drink this lunchtime, and who should be there but Marius and Nadine Winton? Very cosy in a corner of the bar, and far too engrossed in each other to notice me.'

So that was where he had been, Lydie thought with a pang. That was why he hadn't noticed his wet clothes. Because of Nadine. He went from me to her. Oh, dear God...

The years fell away and she was a teenager again, confused and vulnerable, trying to come to terms with emotions she barely understood. With jealousy...

Oh, God, she wept inwardly. Even after everything that's happened, I still care—still hurt. Will I never learn?

She made herself shrug with apparent insouciance. 'They're old friends. And Marius is a free agent,' she added levelly. 'He may do as he wants.'

'He's also a very lucky man,' Hugh sneered. 'A wife not only beautiful but discreetly prepared to look the other way. I never thought you were the long-suffering type, Lydie.'

Long suffering? she screamed at him silently. For five years I've been slowly dying inside, and no one knew. No one...

The smile she sent him was brittle. 'I think,' she said, 'you've been listening to all the wrong rumours.'

'I wish to God you'd listen to me.' Before she could take evasive action he grabbed her, pulling her towards him, seeking her lips with a kind of desperation. 'Oh, Lydie...'

She allowed him to kiss her, standing rigid and un-moving in his embrace, until reluctantly he let her go.

'It's no good, is it?' he said miserably.

'I can't pretend.' Her voice was gentle. 'Not any more. Not about anything. But I wish we could part friends.'

He said stiffly, 'I think that's too much to expect.'

She sighed swiftly and sadly. 'Yes, probably. Well, then—goodbye, Hugh, and good luck.'

She swung herself behind the wheel and drove off. In the mirror she could see his figure, shoulders hunched as if in defeat, watching her departure.

She thought remorsefully, Hugh, I'm sorry—I'm so sorry. I would have been safe with you, and peaceful.

But compassion wasn't love, and nor was security. Instead she'd opted for danger and risk, and all she'd achieved was heartbreak.

She'd gone nearly a mile when she realised she'd turned right instead of left as she'd left the garage and was now driving away from Greystones as hard as she could go. She pressed her foot down on the accelerator. Freudian slip or not, it had served her well. She wasn't ready to go back. Not yet. She needed some time to herself. She had to rethink her life. To plan a future that could only seem unbearably bleak and empty.

Where could she go, after all, and what could she do?

But she mustn't think like that, Lydie castigated herself sharply as she detected the strain of self-pity in her thinking. She had relied for too long on the support of the Benedict name and money. Now she had to jettison the soft option and strike out alone. She was young, healthy and intelligent, and she would survive.

Now, in the short term, she needed a bed for the night.

There was plenty of choice. Some of the more pic-turesque inns were offering accommodation and a number of large country houses locally had turned themselves into hotels, but Lydie passed them by, deciding instead on the comparative anonymity of a modern complex, set down like a concrete box in the middle of the countryside and frankly geared to the needs of company reps and conference trade.

She checked in using her credit card, and was directed to a square room with a double bed, and decor that managed to be bland and offensive at the same time.

The bathroom, on the other hand, was unexpectedly luxurious. The bath was almost big and deep enough to swim in, and it came with baskets of gift toiletries, piles of fluffy towels, and even a complimentary robe.

Lydie stripped off her dress and slip, had a leisurely wash, then wrapped herself in the robe and stretched out on the bed, glancing through the big leather folder advertising the hotel's amenities. There were several bars and three restaurants, she noted, wrinkling her nose dismissively as she turned instead to the room-service menu. The last thing she needed was to be targeted by some lonely-heart salesman trawling for company.

She ordered a pot of coffee and a steak sandwich, which were among the simplest items on offer. She had no real appetite but common sense told her that her inner turmoil would not be assuaged by fasting. Then she dialled reluctantly for an outside line. Her sense of duty dictated that Austin must not be worried by her non-return, but it was a relief when Mrs Arnthwaite answered.

She said quietly, 'Please tell Mr Benedict that I won't be in for dinner. In fact, I won't be back tonight. I—I'm staying with a friend.'

It isn't altogether a lie, she placated her conscience. I may well be the only friend I have.

'Well, I don't know, I'm sure, Miss Lydie.' The housekeeper sounded positively affronted. 'I thought— Mr Benedict said that tonight was going to be a special occasion.' She paused. 'Mr Marius has just come in. Perhaps you'd better have a word—'

'I'm sorry,' Lydie intervened desperately. 'I really have to go.' She replaced the receiver and sat back, her heart thudding unevenly. But at least she'd gained herself a slight respite.

Room service wasn't fast but, rather to her surprise, the sandwich was excellent, the steak juicy and succulent in an enormous floury bun, and the accompanying coffee strong and fragrant. Contrary to expectation, she ate every scrap, and even poured herself a glass of red wine from the room's mini-bar.

When the knock came at the door, she assumed that the waiter had come back for her empty tray.

No delay this time, she thought with a touch of irony as she swung herself off the bed, tightening the belt of her robe.

She carried the tray to the door, balancing it one-handed as she fumbled to turn the knob.

The door opened, and she recoiled with a little cry, the tray spinning from her grasp.

'Bridal nerves, darling?' Marius's tone was harsh as he looked her over. 'Or just a guilty conscience?'

He stepped into the room, pushing the door shut behind him, closing them in together with a kind of terrible finality.

CHAPTER ELEVEN

'WHAT are you doing here?' Lydie's voice sounded hoarse, almost distorted to her own ears.

'I warned you if you ran away I'd follow.'

'But how did you find me?' Her hands twisted together, painfully, betrayingly, before she thrust them into the pockets of the robe.

Marius shrugged. 'It was simple. I just phoned to find the number of the last caller.'

'Of course.' Her tone was hollow.

She dropped to one knee, reaching almost numbly for the scattered crockery and cutlery.

'Leave it.' Marius knelt beside her, piling the used dishes back onto the tray. 'No harm done,' he added, his lip curling slightly. 'The china's thick and so is the carpet. Everything bounced.'

He rose without effort, depositing the tray on the night table, then reached down, lifting Lydie unceremoniously to her feet in turn.

'An odd choice for a romantic rendezvous,' he commented as he glanced round him. 'Or was it the best you could do at short notice?'

'I wasn't planning any kind of rendezvous.' Lydie pulled herself free of his controlling hand. 'I came here to be alone—to think. So I'd be glad if you'd go and leave me in peace.'

'And that's a singularly inappropriate word to choose, too.' There was a steely note in his even tone. 'Don't ever write me off as a fool, Madonna Lily.'

'I won't,' she said. 'There are plenty of other names I'd use first.'

'A game two can play,' he came back grimly. He walked over to the bed and stretched out on it, folding his arms behind his head. 'You don't mind if I make myself comfortable while I wait?'

'Wait for what?' Lydie's voice shook. 'For Hotel Security to come and throw you out? Because that's what will happen if you don't leave now, I swear it.'

'Really?' Marius turned his head and studied her, his eyes contemptuous. 'On what grounds?'

'I've told you—I need to be alone.'

'Let's try a spot of honesty, Lydie,' he suggested tersely. 'We both know you're expecting company. Unless, of course, he's already here, hiding somewhere.'

There was a moment's stunned silence.

'Company?' Lydie repeated slowly. 'Hiding? What the hell are you talking about?'

'I had to go out too this afternoon, as it happens, and on the way back I decided to get some petrol. I was just in time to witness your touching scene with Wingate.' He heard her swift intake of breath and smiled harshly. 'Unlucky for you, darling, and against all the laws of probability, but there it is.'

'I know what you think you saw.' Her words seemed to tumble over themselves. 'But it wasn't like that...'

'Oh, do me a favour, Lydie. The man was kissing you. And you weren't fighting him off either.'

She was about to retort that she hadn't wanted an unpleasant scene to deteriorate even further when it struck her like a bolt of lightning that this could be her way out, her means of escape from an impossible situation.

She hunched a shoulder almost negligently. 'All right—maybe it's true,' she countered. 'Perhaps the last forty-eight hours of blackmail and emotional bullying have made me see Hugh in a new and favourable light.'

Marius sat up, his dark face forged in steel. 'I hope you're not serious,' he said softly.

'Why not?' she flung back defiantly.

'Because you belong to me, Madonna Lily. Body and soul.'

The words sent a tremor through her flesh. 'You can't own another person,' she denied huskily. 'Slavery was abolished long ago.'

'I'm talking about a different kind of enslavement,' he said quietly. 'One where you find yourself bound by chains of sexuality—of emotion. Chains you can't break, however hard you try—however deeply you despise them.'

Her heart thudded with sudden pain. 'Even when one's real obligation is to someone else?' she asked in a low voice.

He shook his head. 'You can't pretend that, Lydie. You turned Wingate down in front of an audience.'

'I wasn't talking about myself.' Her voice was taut as she remembered Darrell Corbin—the overt aggression concealing pain and hurt, her protectiveness towards her child.

Your child, she thought. Oh, Marius...

'But perhaps you're not the only one prepared to overlook my bad behaviour.' Aware of his questioning look, she forced a light tone. 'At least Hugh isn't motivated by revenge. Believe it or not, he wants me for myself.'

'Oh, I believe it,' he returned grittily. 'You're an intensely desirable creature, Madonna Lily, whatever your moral failings.'

'How dare you say that to me?' Her voice shook. 'Your own morality wouldn't bear close scrutiny, Marius. Or did you think I wouldn't find out?'

'Wingate has been busy,' he said harshly. 'But you're barking up the wrong tree, Lydie. There's nothing between Nadine and myself. That was all over long ago.'

She'd assumed that he would realise her reference was to Darrell Corbin, and had to rally herself swiftly. 'Am I supposed to take your word for that?'

'It happens to be the truth.' He swung himself off the bed and walked towards her. 'Pay me the same compliment, Lydie. Are you expecting Wingate to join you in this—down-market love-nest?'

She hesitated only fractionally. 'And what if I am?' she challenged.

'Then he's doomed to disappointment.' The silkiness of his tone didn't deceive her for an instant. He was deeply, powerfully angry. 'But he'll be used to that by now. You can't play straight with any man, my devious angel.'

She shrugged. 'If Hugh's prepared to take the chance, why not let me go to him?'

'Not to him,' he said softly. 'Not to any other man. Not while I live.'

'Oh, please,' Lydie said scornfully. 'Spare me the melodramatics. Why can't you just accept that too much has happened in the past for us ever to have a future? That by punishing me you're simply imposing a life sentence on yourself?'

Her voice broke slightly. 'You don't have to break your chains, Marius. I'm giving you the key. Unlock them and walk away.'

'You're being very eloquent,' he derided. 'You must be getting scared.'

'It's more disgust than fear,' she hit back at him. 'Now, will you please get out, or do I have to get help?'

'You're bluffing, darling,' he drawled. 'I hardly think the hotel would be prepared to exclude your fiancé over a—premarital tiff, shall we say?'

'You can say what you please. It will be my word against yours anyway,' Lydie said shortly. 'And I'm going to make sure I'm believed.'

She took a deep breath. 'Our so-called engagement's over, Marius. See?' She spread bare hands for his inspection.

'Indeed I do,' he said slowly. She saw a muscle flicker at the corner of his mouth. 'So, what did you do with your ring, Lydie—throw it away?'

'Hardly.' She retrieved her bag, fumbling with the zip as she delved for the ring. It felt cold and heavy in her hand. 'One piece of hardware, only slightly used.' She tossed it to him, but he made no attempt to catch it, and it fell to the carpet at his feet.

She went on brightly, 'I'm sure Mr Foxton will give you a full refund. Or you can always save it for a more worthy recipient.'

His eyes never left her face. 'What makes you think I'm prepared to let you go?'

'You have no choice.' She made herself challenge his glittering gaze. 'And no hold over me either. Not any. more.'

'We'll see about that.' The words were quiet, with a steely undertow.

In spite of herself, Lydie found that she was taking a step backwards. Her hands balled into fists in the skirts of the robe as she fought for self-command.

'I won't be threatened,' she said clearly and icily. 'And I won't be emotionally blackmailed. What accusations you've made about me pale into insignificance beside your own behaviour, so come off the moral high ground, Marius. It doesn't suit you.'

She took another swift, uneven breath. 'And, no matter what you say, I don't flatter myself that losing me will cause anything more than a momentary hitch in your single-minded progress.' She swallowed past the tightness in her throat. 'You've turned you back before and walked away—from other people. Try and deny it.'

'No.' He looked her over with unsmiling scorn. 'Let's remember it how it was, Lydie. I was driven away by a tissue of lies, slander and innuendo, in which you played a full part and continue to do so even to this day.'

He took one long, inexorable stride towards her. 'And that's something you can't deny,' he said roughly as he dragged her into his arms. 'Any more than you can deny this.' And he bent his head.

At the first touch of his lips, she recoiled. 'No.'

'You don't have a choice, my sweet.' He was smiling without amusement as he pulled her back to him. 'If this is to be our final parting, I intend to make the most of it.'

His mouth was on hers, sensuous, cynically possessive as he imposed his will on her. In spite of herself, Lydie found herself caught up in the drugging heat of the kiss, felt the raging force inside her, fuelled by anger, spiral passionately out of control.

And even as she began to fight him, beating on his chest with her hands, twisting and turning in his arms, some deeper instinct told her that the battle was over before it had begun. Because she was really fighting herself.

Some profound thrill of consciousness reminded her that this was her man. This was the lover who had sealed his possession of her for good or ill, and for all eternity. The touch, the taste, the scent of him invaded her reeling senses, rendering her oblivious to all but her own burning need. A need that had to be satisfied—at all costs.

Her lips parted slowly beneath his in a silent sigh of acquiescence, and the angry fists slowly uncurled into soft palms that smoothed a path, delicate as swansdown, over his torso to the hard muscularity of his shoulders. She felt the hurried thud of his heartbeat echoing her own as she pressed herself against him.

In instant response to her capitulation, his kiss gentled, deepened into a new and sensual persuasion. One hand cradled the back of her head as his lips began to explore with pulsating urgency the slender line of her throat. His other hand slid to her waist to find the sash of her robe and release it.

She felt breathless, dizzy, every nerve-ending tingling with anticipation as he touched her, his hand moulding her hip in a gesture of male domination, of total ownership. His fingers on her skin, moving slowly upwards across the supple flatness of her stomach to her ribcage, left a trail of flame dancing in their wake.

He cupped her breast, his splayed fingers stroking its fullness, seeking her nipple through the delicate covering of lace as he deliberately used the friction of the material to tantalise the rosy peak and bring it to soaring, aching arousal.

She moaned softly, almost deliriously as the desire to touch him in turn became too great to be borne, and her shaking hands began to fumble the buttons on his shirt free from their holes.

She dragged the edges of the shirt apart, uncaring that she heard it tear as she pressed tiny, frantic kisses over the hair-roughened skin of his chest, her flurried breath rasping in her throat.

Their mouths met again, heatedly, demandingly, his tongue a ribbon of liquid flame against her own.

Her robe fell, disregarded, to the floor. His fingers sought the tiny clasp which fastened her bra, uncovering her slowly, as if it were some sacred ceremony from an ancient, pagan ritual. He caressed each soft, naked mound in turn with hands and lips, circling the erect nipples with his tongue, smiling against her skin as he recognised the deep shudders of delight convulsing her.

She could feel the strength, the potency of his desire against her trembling thighs, meeting it with the satin moisture of her own excitement—her own passionate, inescapable longing. Her blood sang some languorous, siren chant in her ears, stilling the tiny voice which warned that this was wrong, that she was making herself vulnerable to yet more regret, more heartbreak.

And when his hand moved gently to push away the final silky barrier her whole being strained in eagerness and welcome. Her body opened in total candour to the intimacy of his exploration, the skilful, unerring glide of his fingers.

He sank to his knees in front of her, pressing his mouth to the slight concavity of her belly in an act that was almost homage. She felt him breathe, 'Madonna Lily,' against her skin, and her body contracted in a deep shiver of pleasure.

His tongue circled the intricate whorls of her navel then moved slowly downwards. His lips feathered kisses across her pliant thighs, before seeking the throbbing centre of her delight. His hands held her hips, urging her forward to meet the caress as his tongue explored her, flickered against her in overt eroticism.

Lydie could hardly breathe, every nerve-ending, every pulse caught up in the maelstrom of sensation he had created. She was swaying in his embrace like a flower tossed in the wind, eyes blind, ears deaf to everything but the small, imploring, uncontrollable noises being torn from her throat. Her own unspoken pleas for release. For fulfilment.

When, at last, it seemed as if she could bear no more, he swiftly undressed, lifted her into his arms and carried her to the bed.

The sheets were cool, but his body, as he came to lie beside her, burned like fire. A flame that was unutterably, agonisingly familiar.

The years between them seemed to vanish out of existence, and for a few dizzy moments she let herself learn him again, running her hands from his shoulders to the tips of his fingers, from the nape of his neck down the long spine to the flat male buttocks. And finally over the strong thighs to his loins, where her hands found him, held him, worshipped him.

And, as he slid an arm beneath her, lifting her towards him, she guided him surely and joyfully into her.

All the soft, sweet moisture of her enclosed him, held him for one endless, intense moment.

When, eventually, Marius began to move, it was slowly and gently, almost as if he was afraid to break the spell that had them in its thrall.

The rhythm he initiated drew her immediately into its own inexorably deepening pulsation and evoked an equal and passionate response. Her hands gripped his shoulders, her slender legs locking round his hips as their sweat-dampened bodies rose and fell in the timeless patterns of love.

She was one with him. Every fibre of her being seemed concentrated in a relentless spiral upwards to some unseen pinnacle of rapture.

When the climax came, she felt as if she was being torn apart, and her cry of anguished wonder was crushed beneath his kiss as one wild, voluptuous spasm of pleasure succeeded another.

Marius's face was taut, his throat muscles like thick cords as he reared above her. He ground out her name between clenched teeth as he drove powerfully for his own culmination, his body shuddering as it claimed its little death.

As their mutual storm slowly receded, she found that she was clinging to him, her face wet with tears.

His mouth touched her again, licking the salt drops from her cheeks, the tiny pearls of sweat from her breasts. Lydie lay pliant, her hand stroking his hair, as she savoured the delicacy of this new sensation. Discovered too, with a sense of shock, that she found it gently, insidiously arousing. Realised too that Marius's fingers were insinuating a path between her thighs. And that, far from being sated, the core of her womanhood was opening to him once more in offering as he caressed her.

Her eyes widened in sudden disquiet. In disbelief. She tried to frame a protest through numb lips—attempted to push away that expertly marauding hand. And felt him smile against her skin as he forestalled her, capturing her wrists in his other hand and pinioning them unhurriedly above her head.

He said softly, 'Oh, no, my sweet. You don't escape that easily.' He kissed her mouth slowly and thoroughly, tracing the faint swelling of her lower lip with his tongue. 'We have a long way to go yet. A very long way indeed.'

At some point on the journey, her body racked with fresh paroxysms of delight, she heard him say, 'This is the only reality, Lydie. So God help us both.'

The bed was a cloud, drawing her down, enveloping her in its softness. Her eyelids felt as if they had lead weights attached to them. In some dim recess of her mind she was aware of movement, of vague sounds, one of which might have been a door softly closing, but, exhausted by pleasure, Lydie burrowed deeper into her cloud, and slept on as if she had been drugged.

It was morning before she stirred, and sunlight was pouring through the half-closed drapes. She lay still for a moment, savouring the almost miraculous sense of wellbeing which pervaded her entire body, then turned, reaching out a drowsy hand across the bed to Marius, only to encounter the chill of emptiness.

As if some alarm had sounded, her eyes flew open, and she sat up, propping herself dazedly on her elbow, and stared around her, pushing back her tumbled hair.

But the room was empty—the space beside her in bed unoccupied.

She remembered the quiet noises she'd heard, and looked hopefully towards the closed bathroom door. Perhaps he'd gone for a shower. She listened intently for the sound of running water, but there was only silence.

In spite of the warmth of the room, Lydie felt suddenly very cold. She got out of bed and retrieved the robe, still lying crumpled on the floor with her underclothes. As she was tying the sash, she saw the envelope propped against the lamp on the dressing table.

The sheet of paper inside bore two laconic sentences. 'It was a memorable parting. Goodbye, Madonna Lily, and good luck.' It wasn't even signed.

She stood staring down at his handwriting, feeling the words burn into her brain.

So that was it. All over and finished with, courtesy of a piece of hotel notepaper. A bubble of something like laughter welled up inside her and emerged as a sob.

But this is what you wanted, an inexorable voice in her brain reminded her. This is what you actually demanded, hours ago, in some previous existence.

You knew that you could have no future with Marius. That Darrell Corbin and her child would always stand in the way. You knew, as well, that he's probably never given her a second thought from that day to this. How could you have imagined, even for a moment, that he would treat you any differently?

Because she'd fallen into the eternal trap for unwary women, she told herself as tears pricked savagely at her eyelids. Because she'd let herself believe the age-old myth that her love would somehow transform the man she wanted into a prince.

Because she'd hoped—prayed even—that, against all the evidence, he would indeed be different with her.

So, even knowing what Marius was, she had still fallen into his arms—allowed him to take her to paradise during one endless night. Nothing could change that—or excuse it.

She'd behaved like a pathetic, lovesick fool, and now she had to live with that, and bear the consequences. And all she could pray was that they would prove to be solely emotional and not physical. Forging a new life for herself, establishing a new identity would be hard enough without the burden of single parenthood to weight her down.

It was the future she had to focus on now—channelling her energies towards some kind of new horizon. Though what it might be she could not even hazard a guess. All the delicious lassitude of her awakening had been transmuted into a profound and desolate weariness.

It took all the strength and self-control she possessed not to sink onto the ground and weep for love and its betrayal, as if she was mourning a death. Which perhaps she was.

But there was no time for grieving now. She had plans to make—her departure to organise.

And maybe there would come a moment when she would realise at last that Marius wasn't worth the shedding of one solitary tear, and never had been. And, from that point, she would be able to begin the rest of her life in earnest.

But that, she admitted wretchedly, as shame joined with the pain inside her, was no consolation now, when she loved him and wanted him as much as ever. Or even more.

CHAPTER TWELVE

LYDIE showered like an automaton, standing motionless while the cascade of hot water pounded over her. She might rid herself of his touch, his scent, but the cleansing power of the water could not wipe away the memory of his caresses, the huskiness of his voice as he'd worshipped her beauty, or the faint marks of passion imprinted on her naked skin.

Nor could she forget how shamingly easily she had surrendered. How could she, in all conscience, despise Marius for his utter lack of principle when she had just proved herself to be no better?

Shuddering, she turned off the water and wrapped herself in one of the enormous bath sheets that the hotel provided. If only it were a cloak of invisibility, she thought desperately, which would allow her to vanish without a trace.

Instead, with a fastidious grimace, she had to redress herself in yesterday's clothes, using the pocket comb in her bag to restore her dishevelled hair to some kind of order.

As she was about to leave, she suddenly remembered how she had flung her ring at Marius's feet. A swift scan of the carpet revealed nothing and she dropped to her knees to peer under the bed and dressing table.

But there was no sign of the ring anywhere. Marius had apparently taken her strictly at her word, and, in spite of herself, she felt oddly chilled.

There was a rattle at the door and a chambermaid entered, arms laden with bedding and clean towels. She checked in surprise when she saw Lydie.

'Sorry, madam. I thought the room had been vacated.'

'Yes.' Lydie scrambled to her feet. 'Of course, it should have been. I was just going when I realised I'd lost something—an earring . . .' Her voice trailed away as she saw the girl's eyes rest pointedly on the pearl studs safe and well in her ears, and she felt herself flush in vexed embarrassment.

'All lost property is handed in to management, madam.' The chambermaid moved towards the bathroom. 'You could always ring the hotel tomorrow, or call.'

She had one more humiliation to endure. When she arrived at Reception and asked for her bill, the girl, her eyes sharp with speculation, told her that it had been paid already and handed back her credit-card slip, torn neatly in half.

I feel like a call-girl, Lydie thought angrily as she wheeled away from the desk and marched, head high, towards the main swing-doors. I suppose I should be glad he didn't actually leave some money on the night table.

She sat for a while in the car park, staring ahead of her, silently oblivious to the comings and goings of other vehicles, her mind turning slowly and painfully on her immediate problems.

She should, she knew, go back to Greystones. She needed at least some of her clothes and possessions before she walked away from her old life for ever.

But Marius might still be there too, and she felt too raw, too fragile to risk another meeting with him so soon.

But there was another confrontation which could not be delayed any longer, she decided grimly as she started the Corsa and headed it towards Wheeldon Grange.

The reception area of the health farm was all elegant pastels, with strains of Vivaldi's *Four Seasons* playing discreetly in the background.

The girl behind the desk shared the muted chic of her surroundings. Perfect teeth were bared in an enquiring smile. 'Madam has a reservation?'

Lydie shook her head. 'I have to see Mrs Benedict urgently,' she said. 'She's my mother.'

The girl consulted a computer screen and nodded. 'She is expecting you, madam. The Blue Suite on the first floor, if you'd like to go up.'

Expecting me? Lydie bit back the surprised query, merely nodding and turning away towards the broad, shallow flight of stairs.

She knocked at the door of Debra's suite and heard her mother say, 'Come in,' her voice sharply edged.

Lydie found herself in a small but luxurious sitting room. As the name suggested, the predominating colour in curtains and furnishings was blue, including even the robe that Debra wore and the silky turban her hair was swathed in. Standing by the sunlit window, she made a striking picture.

She stared at Lydie, her hand going to her throat. 'What the hell are you doing here?'

'I thought you were anticipating a visit?' Lydie returned, her voice even.

'Not from you,' Debra said, with a small sob. 'From Jon.' Without make-up, her face was naked, vulnerable.

Of course, Lydie thought wearily, stifling an instinctive pang of sympathy. Not me. Never me. But this time she's not getting away with it.

She said coolly, 'I'd have thought Jon had enough problems at the mill without paying social calls during working hours.'

'Working hours?' Debra's shrill laugh held a touch of hysteria. 'That's rich—when he's just been sacked. Oh, yes.' She nodded fiercely at Lydie's astonished expression. 'That's been his reward for working himself into the ground for the Benedicts all these years. Instant dismissal.' She lifted a shaking hand and pressed it to her mouth. 'He rang me here an hour ago—more—to say he'd been told to clear his desk. He sounded—terrible—like a stranger.'

Lydie bit her lip. 'I don't think it can have come as that much of a shock. Jon was quite aware that he hadn't been a resounding success as sales director. This could be the shot in the arm he needs to get his life and future together.'

'With your hippy girlfriend, I suppose.' Debra glared at her. 'You're talking like a complete fool. Where on earth is Jon going to get anything like the same position—the same salary—once it's known he's been fired from Benco? This is all the doing of your precious fiancé, of course,' she added furiously. 'He hates Jon for taking his place, and this is his revenge.'

Could it be true? Lydie wondered. Was this Marius's way of exacting an eye for an eye? And would a tooth for a tooth follow? It didn't bear thinking about.

She swallowed. 'I hope very much that you're wrong about that.'

'Of course that's what it is.' Debra waved a dismissive hand. 'But he's not getting away with it. You've got to talk to him, Lydie. Make him see that Jon deserves another chance.'

Lydie shook her head. 'I'm sorry, but I can't do that.'

'What?' Debra's eyes blazed at her. 'You mean you take that—that creature's side against your own brother?'

Lydie drew a deep breath. 'It's not a question of taking sides,' she said flatly. 'The fact is I no longer have any influence with Marius.' If I ever did, she added silently. 'We—ended our engagement last night. That's one of the things I came here to tell you.'

'You've broken off your engagement?' Debra's voice dropped to a harsh whisper. 'Are you completely crazy?'

'On the contrary, I think I'm hanging onto my sanity by a whisker,' Lydie retorted. 'Don't tell me you're sorry, Mother. Don't add hypocrisy to everything else.'

'How dare you talk to me like that?' Debra stiffened in outrage.

Lydie sighed. 'No more pretence, please. I know exactly what you did five years ago. I know how you got rid of Marius.'

'What are you talking about?' Debra was suddenly ashen.

'I'm talking about the lies you told Austin about him— about us.' Her voice broke. 'Mother, how could you? Don't you realise you almost destroyed me?'

'You were little more than a child. You didn't—you couldn't know your own mind.' Debra's tone was feverish, her eyes almost blank. 'I saw you go to him that night. I couldn't sleep and I watched you walking down the passage to his room. I told myself I should stop you— but I didn't. It was a God-given opportunity to turn Austin against Marius for good. To make him believe that you were a victim of abuse—of rape, but too ashamed to speak about it yourself.

'I knew Marius would write to you, so I instructed the school to intercept all letters except mine. I even had that note you'd written to me with the bursar's bill for your extra art lessons—the one where you said you thought Austin should deal with it. And he played right into my hands.'

Her tiny laugh was, in spite of everything, almost exultant. 'It all fitted perfectly. The one sin that I knew Austin couldn't forgive. Because you were family.'

'That's sick,' Lydie said with passion, and Debra glanced at her as if surprised.

'But I had to be sure.' She sounded as if she was offering a reasonable explanation. 'Unless I got rid of Marius, there was no real chance for Jon. You must see that.'

'And what about my chance?' Lydie spoke quietly and desolately. 'I loved Marius. You broke my heart.'

'Hearts are soon mended,' Debra said harshly. 'If that bastard hadn't come back you'd be planning your wedding to Hugh by now. As it is, you've lost both of them. I wash my hands of you.'

'You can't do that. You're not playing the sleepwalking scene from the Scottish play, Mother.' Lydie grasped Debra's arms through the thin robe and shook her gently. 'This is reality, and you have to face it.'

Just as I've done, she thought, her whole being wincing away from the hurt of it.

For a moment there was silence, then Debra said haltingly, 'Does he—know? Have you told Marius the truth?'

'No,' Lydie said quietly, torn between pity and contempt. 'No, I wouldn't do that. I let him go on thinking it was me.'

'Thank God.' Debra gave a shuddering sigh. She pulled herself free and sat down on one of the thickly padded brocade armchairs. Her face beneath the blue turban looked haggard. 'Because he'd tell his uncle—he'd be bound to—and Austin must never find out what I've done. I couldn't bear it, Lydie.' Her eyes were suddenly enormous with tears. 'It would be the end of everything—and I love Austin—I really do.'

Lydie gave her a level look. 'I hope you mean that. Judging by your remarks a couple of evenings ago, I'd begun to wonder.'

'Oh—that.' Debra's shrug was almost airy. 'I was upset by Marius's return.'

'And with good reason,' Lydie said drily. She paused. 'But you're not out of the wood yet. Sooner or later the truth's bound to come out. So why don't you go to Austin yourself—tell him everything?'

'Oh, but I couldn't.' Some colour crept into her mother's pale face. 'I couldn't risk it. He would never be able to understand. He has such high standards himself...'

With a pang, Lydie remembered Darrell Corbin's set, defiant face, her justifiable bitterness at her treatment by the Benedict men. 'He might be more sympathetic than you think,' she said quietly. 'Maybe he hasn't always behaved as well as he might in order to—protect someone.'

Debra shrugged pettishly. 'If you believe that, darling, then you don't know Austin.' She sighed. 'But perhaps I don't know him very well either—if he's allowed Jon to be summarily dismissed like that. He must have known how it would upset me.'

He'd also known how she'd feel about Marius returning, but that hadn't stopped him either, Lydie reminded herself uneasily.

She said, 'I really think you should go back to Greystones, Mother, and get a few things sorted out.'

'I shall do nothing of the kind.' Debra's chin tilted mutinously. 'And you can tell Austin from me that I have no intention of going home until Jon is fully reinstated.'

Lydie shook her head. 'I shall be telling Austin nothing, because I'm going away myself.'

'Going away?' Debra echoed. 'But where—and why?'

'I haven't decided where yet—or when. I shall have to make arrangements with Nell over the future of the gallery.' How calm she sounded, and practical, whereas in reality her stomach was churning and she wanted very badly to put her head in her mother's lap and cry her eyes out. Only, they'd never had that kind of relationship, and common sense told her that they never would. 'As to why, I should have thought that was self-evident.'

'But you can't do this,' Debra wailed. 'You can't simply clear out, leaving all this mess. After all, it's probably entirely your fault that Jon's lost his job.'

When she'd recovered her breath, Lydie asked evenly, 'How on earth do you figure that?'

Debra shrugged again. 'You've broken your engagement. Marius is obviously getting his own back and poor Jon is the sufferer.'

Lydie set her jaw. 'Then, if I'm really the cause of so much aggravation, the best I can do is remove myself.'

'No.' Debra beat the arm of her chair with a clenched fist. 'You've got to go to Marius and persuade him to see reason. Make up this quarrel you've had with him for all our sakes. We have to stick together now. You must see that.'

Lydie shook her head. 'Sorry, Mother, but I can't do that. I can't go on paying the price for other people's lies—other people's silences.'

She bent and dropped a light kiss on Debra's averted cheek. 'I'll be in touch as soon as I've made some plans.'

'Do as you please.' Debra tossed her turbaned head. 'But I'm shocked, Lydie. I never believed you could be so selfish.'

And with those words ringing in her head Lydie went down to the car.

In spite of her avowed intention to dissociate herself from the family problems, she drove straight to Thornshaugh and parked in her usual spot behind the gallery.

She was surprised not to find Jon's car there too. But, after all, it was a company car. Maybe it had been taken away from him along with the job, she thought with a faint grimace.

For the first time since they'd started the gallery, Lydie found herself climbing the stairs with reluctance. How could she break the news to Nell that she was leaving? she wondered sadly. And what reason could she give that wouldn't involve embarrassing or damaging explanations?

To her astonishment, she found the gallery locked and the 'Closed' notice in place. Another and equally disturbing first, she thought as she rooted in her bag for her own set of keys.

For a moment, she thought the place was totally deserted, then she heard sounds of movement from Nell's studio and her friend appeared in the doorway.

Lydie suppressed a gasp. Nell's usually tranquil air had been shattered. She was white-faced, her eyes redrimmed and heavy as if she hadn't slept.

Lydie said urgently, 'Nell—what is it, love? Have you been ill?'

Nell shook her head. She said huskily, 'I've been trying to phone you—only Mrs Arnthwaite didn't know where you were.'

'No, I spent the night away from home.' Lydie took a step towards her. 'Is it—Jon?' she queried gently.

Nell nodded convulsively. 'It's been such a shock, Lydie. I don't know what to do. I—I didn't open this morning because I've been packing. I've got to get away for a few days—to think. To try to put things in some kind of perspective. Would you be able to cope on your own until I get back?'

'Why, yes, of course.' Lydie felt utterly bewildered. Nell had always wanted Jon to be free of Benco. Did the means of his release really matter that much to her?

She said carefully, 'Will Jon be going with you?'

'No.' The word cut the air like a knife. 'I won't have him anywhere near me—not after what he's done. You may be able to make allowances for him, Lydie, but I can't.'

Lydie swallowed. These were deep waters suddenly. What on earth had Jon done to cause such a violent reaction from the girl who loved him? Surely nothing criminal, she thought with horror. She tried to think back to the brief conversation they'd had. He'd spoken of mistakes but, surely, nothing worse than that?

'It's not just the financial side of it,' Nell went on, her voice trembling. 'I could cope with that—somehow. It's the deceit—the total heartlessness—' She broke off, shaking her head. 'You must understand how I feel.'

Lydie drew a breath. 'Yes—yes, of course.' If only she *did*. She hesitated for a moment, her mind in turmoil. 'Would you like me to go with you, Nell? I don't think you should be on your own right now.'

'Being alone,' Nell said, with a small, painful smile, 'is something I'm going to have to get used to. Don't worry about me. I'll make it.' She looked at Lydie, her brow wrinkling. 'But all this must be affecting you badly too, love. I was so full of my own problems, I didn't think about that.'

Lydie smiled resolutely. 'As a matter of fact, I was going to ask a big favour. Could I stay here—use the studio while you're away? I have some sorting out of

my own to do.' She paused. 'And when you come back
we'll have to talk seriously about the future.'

'Yes,' Nell said flatly, 'I'm afraid we will.' She put
her arms round Lydie and gave her a quick, fierce hug.
'You can stay as long as you want—you know that.'
There were tears in her eyes as she turned away. 'Oh,
Lydie, I'm so sorry. It's all such a ghastly mess.'

The gallery seemed very silent and very empty after
she'd gone. Lydie put the kettle on and made herself a
mug of strong black coffee. The sun was pouring in
through the gallery windows. It was going to be a hot
day, but she felt deathly cold. Nell's words haunted her.
'Not just the financial side...the deceit—the total
heartlessness—' Could Jon possibly have been embez-
zling money from the mill? The very idea made her feel
quite sick.

I should have made her tell me, she thought broodingly. Only she seemed to think that I knew. That I could
even be ready to condone his behaviour. And, besides,
she was too distressed for a cross-examination.

She sighed. When Nell returned, there would have to
be some straight talking. She laced her fingers round the
mug and waited for the inner trembling to go away.

It helped when the first customers of the day began
arriving. She had to close off all the desperate questions
whirling in her brain and concentrate on attending to
them. Normally, she'd have been jubilant, recording
several excellent sales on a Monday when business was
usually slow. But nothing seemed to matter any more
except the bleakness and emptiness inside her.

Hanging over her was the knowledge that she would
have to go back to Greystones to collect at least some
of her belongings.

The lunch-hour would probably be the best time, she
decided reluctantly, although it would mean closing the

gallery. But at least she'd be unlikely to find anyone else at the house. Even Mrs Arnthwaite would be absent, on her weekly visit to her sister in Huddersfield.

All the same, she felt like a thief in the night as she quietly let herself into the house a few hours later.

She went straight to her room. She would take just the minimum necessary for the next few days and send for the rest of her things when she'd established some kind of plan for the future.

She shivered. At the moment that seemed totally impossible to contemplate. But maybe that was because Greystones had represented safety and security for so many years. Even when Marius had been away, the fact that she was there, in his home, surrounded by memories, had given her a kind of comfort.

But I shouldn't have settled for that, she told herself raggedly. I shouldn't have kept silent. I should have kicked up a fuss—demanded answers to all those questions. There'd have been trouble, yes, when the truth came out, but at least it wouldn't have festered all these years—become this secret monster we're all so scared of.

Now here she was, caught between the rock of her love for Marius and the hard place of her loyalty to her mother.

The price of silence was a bitter one indeed.

She swung her case off the bed and walked to the door. She was halfway down the stairs when the front door opened and Marius walked in.

Lydie checked, dismay sweeping through her. For a moment she hesitated, her hand tightening round the handle of her case, then she continued her descent, her face a mask of cool composure.

His face gave nothing away, but there was something in his stance, an unmistakable tension in his lean body, which communicated itself to her across the space dividing them. She saw his hands clenched into fists at his sides, and knew instinctively, warily that the immaculately cut business suit, the snowy shirt and silk tie were only a civilised veneer covering something far more primitive, and dangerously near to running out of control.

He said, 'Making your getaway, Lydie?'

'I'm leaving, yes.' She kept her voice even. 'I wasn't expecting to run into anyone. The house is usually empty at this time.'

'But this,' he said softly, 'is turning into a very unusual day all round. I imagine you've heard the news about Jon?'

'Yes.' She looked down at the rich colours of the carpet.

'And you've nothing to say about it?' There was a note of faint derision in his voice. 'No last-minute pleas for his reinstatement?'

'I think they'd be pointless.' She lifted her chin, forcing herself to meet his gaze. 'I suppose Jon's departure was inevitable, but did it have to be quite so sudden—and so public? There's bound to be talk.'

He shrugged. 'Just as there was about me five years ago,' he reminded her ironically. 'Does he somehow deserve more consideration?'

'Actually, I was thinking of Nell,' she retorted. 'She's been totally devastated by the news—and she certainly doesn't deserve it.'

'No.' His mouth twisted. 'Believe it or not, she has my sympathy. But in any war, as I said, there are bound to be casualties.'

'*War?*' Lydie echoed with disbelief. 'Is that how you regard the last few days?'

'No,' he said. 'The last ten years. Ever since Austin brought you all to live here. I wanted peaceful coexistence, but of course that wouldn't do. And by the time I'd realised what a powerful and persistent enemy I'd acquired it was too late.' His mouth moved in a smile that was more a grimace. 'You were the joker in the pack, Lydie. I thought you were on my side. You had me totally fooled.'

She was shaking again inwardly, but she took a step forward, her eyes going past him to the open door. 'Well, now we all know where we stand. I hope you're content with that.'

'Oh, no.' Marius shook his head. 'Nothing but total victory will do. I've been promising myself that for the last five years.'

Her heart sank. 'I suppose there's no way I can dissuade you...?'

The mockery in his laugh laid a whip across her senses. 'What did you have in mind, Madonna Lily? The occasional use of that charming body of yours as compensation for what you and your family did to me? Thanks, but no. I sated myself with you last night. From now on I'll be looking for a change of diet.'

The whip lashed her again. Before she could stop herself, she said, 'Nadine Winton, I presume.'

'Among others,' he drawled. 'Why? I hope you're not going to preach morality to me, darling. You're hardly in any position to do so.'

'And, as I've said before, you're no candidate for the moral high ground either,' she flung at him. 'I suppose the name Darrell Corbin still occupies some vague corner of your memory?'

His head went back and his eyes narrowed. He said silkily, 'Better than that, she had a meeting with me at the mill this morning.'

'How noble of you,' Lydie said scornfully. 'Have you decided to take some responsibility for her at last?'

'No. I don't think she'd welcome it. She seems to have developed remarkable self-sufficiency since I saw her last.'

Lydie gasped. 'Is that all you can say?' she demanded wildly. 'Don't you care about the way she's been treated?'

'I regret that I didn't look for her and get the whole mess sorted out five years ago,' Marius said tersely. 'But I doubt that's what you want to hear.'

'No—no, it isn't.' Lydie's throat constricted almost unbearably. 'Marius—she has a child. A child without a father.'

'Yes.' He paused, then said reluctantly, 'I'll make sure proper maintenance is paid from now on. Will that satisfy you, perhaps?'

'It's a start.' She couldn't believe that he was talking like this—dismissing his own son. 'But I doubt it will satisfy Darrell Corbin. She—she still cares, Marius. Surely that should be of some concern?'

'It's unfortunate,' he allowed curtly.

'And that's all?' He was a stranger, facing her against a rapidly widening gulf. She couldn't reach him any more. And maybe she shouldn't even want to try.

'Oh, for God's sake.' His voice was suddenly raw. 'What the hell did she expect—love and marriage? It was never going to happen, and you know that as well as I do.'

'I don't think I know anything any more.' She was suddenly very tired, and sick—sick to her stomach with disillusionment. Was this the real Marius? Had the tender lover of her girlhood been just a sham after all?

She said bitterly, 'There's no end to all this hurting. It just goes on and on.'

'Life's a bitch and then you die.' He moved aside, gesturing towards the open door. 'On your way, Lydie.

Maybe, once we're apart for good, we can both start to heal.'

For a moment she stared at him in disbelief, then she walked slowly past him, the case a ton weight in her hand. She was close enough to feel the warmth of his body, but he made no attempt to reach for her, and the knowledge of how much she craved his touch for one last time made her writhe inwardly.

From the doorway she swung to face him as rage and grief, mingled with shame, welled up inside her in a deadly mixture.

'I hope you never heal—you bastard.' Her voice cracked. 'Oh, God, I hope you bleed to death for ever and ever.'

His face was weary, the lines beside his mouth more deeply etched. In spite of her storm of emotion, Lydie thought with a pang, This is how he'll look when he's old—and I won't be there...

He said, 'I'm sure your prayer will be answered, Madonna Lily. In fact, I think the process has already started.'

The door closed behind her, softly but quite inexorably, and Lydie found herself standing in the glare of the afternoon sun, more alone and more frightened than she had ever been in her life.

CHAPTER THIRTEEN

LYDIE was thankful for the gallery that day. Almost as soon as she got back there, another determined trickle of tourists began arriving, giving her no time to think—to brood.

At the end of the afternoon the takings were more than satisfactory. Ironic, Lydie thought, if the business started a real boom now, when circumstances were forcing her to abandon it.

She was just about to lock up when Jon walked in.

Her heart sank at the sight of him, but she managed a calm smile and a word of greeting which he didn't seem to hear. Instead, he stood staring round him like a lost soul.

'Do you know where she's gone?' He was very pale, his eyes desperate.

Lydie sighed. 'No—she wouldn't tell me.' She led the way to the studio. 'You'd better sit down and I'll make some coffee.'

'Not for me.' He subsided onto a chair. 'I could do with a real drink.'

'You smell as if you've already had one,' Lydie said curtly.

He gave her a subdued glare. 'For God's sake, Lydie. My life is already in ruins. I don't need the heavy-sister act.'

'Then perhaps you'd better tell me exactly what's been going on during the past twenty-four hours.'

'What did Nell say?' He sounded wary.

'She wasn't making a great deal of sense.' Lydie frowned. 'But I gathered there was some ghastly mess involving money.' She paused. 'Jon—I have to ask this— is it going to be a police matter?'

'*Police?*' he uttered explosively. 'Of course not. What the hell do you take me for?'

'At the moment, I'm not sure. Certainly a fool, possibly worse,' she hit back. 'I want the truth, Jon, and I want it now. I've had all the lies I can take.'

He didn't look at her. 'We'd had such a wonderful day,' he said in a muffled voice. 'We—we'd really missed each other. In the evening we were going out for a drink, only Nell said she was expecting a visitor—a local artist whose work you'd been handling, but who was leaving the area and wanted to collect her unsold stuff.'

Lydie felt as if cold fingers had touched the back of her neck. She said, 'Go on.'

He said, 'I was in here when I heard the doorbell chime, and then Nell talking to someone.'

He ran his tongue round his lips. His voice was hoarse. 'I went out—and *she* was standing there. Lydie, it was like a bad dream. I'd never expected to see her again— never wanted to—yet here she was.'

He shook his head dazedly. 'I knew she painted, of course, because that was how it all started—with me running into her up on the moors while I was home for the Easter vac—but I hadn't the least idea she'd returned.'

There was almost a note of self-pity in his voice. 'Why the hell did she have to come back? She was paid to stay away. And why did she choose this place to sell her bloody paintings? Of all the filthy, lousy luck...' He buried his head in his hands.

'Oh, dear God.' Lydie barely breathed the words through stiff lips. 'You're talking about Darrell Corbin.'

'Of course I am.' He looked up at her, his eyes haunted. 'It was hideous. I couldn't think straight—didn't know what to say—what to do. Darrell was standing there like some figure of Nemesis, with Nell—my Nell—looking at the pair of us. Putting two and two together and coming up with all the right answers.'

'Darrell Corbin had your baby,' Lydie whispered. 'And you paid her to go away so that you could put the blame on Marius. It—it's unbelievable—monstrous.'

'It wasn't my idea,' Jon said defensively. 'It was Mama's. Old man Corbin came steaming up to the house to see Austin and blow the whistle on me, only he got Mother instead, and she persuaded him to do a deal. A lump sum for Darrell and a regular allowance payable to Percy, in return for pointing the finger at Marius and then keeping out of the way.' His mouth twisted. 'That was in the days when life with Austin was practically a blank cheque.

'Originally, Mama wanted Darrell to have an abortion, but she refused point-blank. However, she did eventually agree to move away. And she'd no idea about the deal Mama had made with her father. At least, not then. She believed the money was from me—a kind of kiss-off payment—so she probably wasn't too sorry to go.'

'No,' Lydie said levelly, 'I can imagine.'

'And Mama picked the right man in Corbin. He was always short of cash, and Marius had sacked him from the mill for boozing on the night shift anyway, so he was looking to get his own back.'

He gave her a shamefaced glance. 'He repeated to Austin exactly what Mama had told him to say, and all hell broke loose. The rest you know.'

'Yes,' Lydie said quietly, her heart like a stone. 'Only too well.'

'Come off it, Lydie. Don't play the innocent. You must have been in on this too at some point.' Jon sounded almost resentful. 'Darrell said you'd been to see her. I suppose Mama found out somehow that she was around again and sent you with another pay-off.'

'Then you're wrong,' Lydie flung at him. 'Actually, I took her a cheque for the pictures we'd sold here.' She gave a small, savage laugh. 'But she thought the same as you. No wonder she threw it back in my face.' She paused, frowning. 'She can't have known, though, that you and Nell were involved—not until yesterday.'

'She had no idea,' Jon confirmed wretchedly. 'Selling her work here was just a ghastly coincidence.'

'What goes around comes around,' Lydie said quietly. 'You and Mama must have been crazy to think this would stay under wraps indefinitely.' She sighed. 'I suppose all we can do is pray Austin never finds out. Not that Mama deserves it, but—'

'It's too late for that,' Jon muttered. 'When Percy Corbin ended up in the hospice a few weeks ago, he asked Austin to visit him. I guess his conscience was troubling him, because he told him everything.'

'Oh, no.' Lydie stared at him, appalled. 'No, that can't be true.'

'Why else do you think Austin brought Marius back like that?' Jon demanded irritably. 'As soon as they sent for me this morning, I knew I was for it.'

Lydie looked at him disdainfully. 'I hope you're not claiming wrongful dismissal.'

'Hardly.' Jon made a wry face. 'Anyway, I haven't actually been sacked—just severely demoted. Marius offered me a junior post in the design department—presumably so that I've no excuse for evading my child-support responsibilities,' he added bitterly.

'But what's going to happen to Mama?' Lydie's voice was urgent.

Jon shrugged. 'Who knows? Austin didn't exactly take me into his confidence, but he was looking pretty grim.'

'Aren't you worried about her?' Lydie demanded.

Jon set his jaw. 'My only concern, frankly, is Nell.' He shuddered. 'God, Lydie, I've never seen her like that—so cold—so angry. She looked at me as if I'd just crawled out of a garbage bin. She said she never wanted to see me again.'

'I know how she felt.' Lydie's voice bit. 'Whatever Mama did, Jon, no matter how wrong it was, she did for you. She wanted you to have Benco Mill, and because of it she could have lost everything, including her marriage.'

Jon's shoulders slumped. 'I know,' he admitted unhappily. 'But there was nothing we could do. From the moment Marius came back we've been waiting for the axe to fall. Now that it's happened, it's almost a relief.'

'And to hell with the innocent victims who happen to have got in the way.' Lydie shivered, wrapping her arms round her body. 'I think you'd better go, Jon. I need to think.'

'All right,' he acquiesced reluctantly, and got to his feet. 'Tim Broughton's putting me up for the time being. If—when Nell comes back, will you let me know?'

'If that's what she wants.' Lydie walked with him to the gallery door, waiting to lock it behind him. 'And only if.'

'But I love her.' He looked at her imploringly. 'I can't lose her, Lydie. I couldn't bear it.'

Lydie hardened her heart. 'Then it's a pity you couldn't be honest with her at least,' she retorted. 'And I wouldn't count on a thing. Nell has integrity, brother, dear.

Something you can't even spell,' she added scathingly to his retreating back.

Alone once more, she made herself tidy the gallery and count the day's takings, ready for banking in the morning. But the totals kept coming out wrong, and eventually she pushed her paperwork aside and sat staring into space.

Work was no answer to the ache, the shivering, nauseous emptiness inside her.

She needed Marius—to warm her and make her complete again—and she could not have him. Their final parting had been made and there was no going back. She had to come to terms with that, however heart-wrenching it might be.

He had come back for his revenge, and she was part of it—no more than that. And it was what she deserved.

Because she hadn't trusted him sufficiently. Because she'd been too much of a coward to fight for him against the tissue of lies that had been woven around their relationship. Because she'd been afraid to demand the truth. Because she'd been all too easily deceived. She should have known, beyond reason, beyond all doubt, that the Marius she had grown up to love was incapable of that kind of treachery.

She thought, When he left, I should have followed him—to the ends of the earth, if necessary. All these years I've been accusing him of betraying me but I was the real Judas.

And then, desolately, It's all my fault, and I deserve to lose him—but, dear God, it hurts so much. And tears, scalding and salt, filled her eyes and her mouth, and ran down the hands she pressed against her face.

She was grieving for Marius, and the death of the love she had helped to kill.

'Oh, darling,' she whispered in anguish. 'Forgive me—please.'

And heard her words dissolve, unanswered, into the unrelenting silence surrounding her.

She cried for a long time, until she had no more tears to shed. She sat for a time feeling numb, shell-shocked, as if some bomb had erupted, leaving her among its wreckage.

Then, when she had regained sufficient composure, she picked up the phone and called Wheeldon Grange.

She'd lost her own love, she told herself bleakly, but it might still not be too late to save her mother's relationship with Austin, or at least to warn her that her fragile world was about to come crashing down around her.

But when she asked for Debra she was told that Mrs Benedict had cancelled the rest of her stay and returned home. And, yes, her departure had been rather unexpected, but her husband had arrived to collect her.

'Some domestic problem, I believe, Miss Hatton,' added the smooth voice at the other end of the phone.

So that's that, Lydie thought wearily, replacing the receiver.

She sat for a while, drumming her fingers restlessly on the table, wondering what she should do. But she knew the answer to that already. Debra was in trouble and needed her—or needed someone, she amended wryly as she splashed her face with water to remove the traces of her emotional trauma. No doubt she'd prefer Jon, but he was too wrapped up in his own problems to help his mother.

She had no idea what she was going to say—what kind of plea she could enter on Debra's behalf. What possible excuse could you make to a man whose wife had told him so many monstrous lies?

How could she ever convince Austin that Debra deserved forgiveness at any level, let alone a second chance? And was it even true?

I simply don't know, she thought. I only know I have to try.

She changed hurriedly into jeans and a sleeveless top, tied a sweater around her shoulders against the coolness of the evening, and grabbed up her bag and car keys.

It was twilight when she arrived at the house, but there were no lights on inside that she could see. Lydie ran up the steps and tried the door, finding it unlocked.

There was a deep hush everywhere. The drawing room and dining room were both deserted, she realised uneasily.

Lydie went quickly and quietly up the stairs. As she reached her mother's door it opened and Mrs Arnthwaite emerged, carrying a bundle of dirty linen.

She gave a muffled squeak and dropped her burden. 'Gracious heavens, Miss Lydie, you're enough to frighten anyone out of their wits, creeping about like that. I thought you were off staying with friends.'

'I was.' Lydie swiftly buried her ringless hand in her jeans pocket. 'But I needed to see my mother. Is she somewhere about?'

'Indeed she isn't, miss.' The housekeeper sounded astonished. 'Why, she left hours ago.'

Lydie swallowed. 'I—see. Did she say when she was coming back?' Or even if? she added silently.

'No, miss, but she'll be gone a while, judging by the amount of luggage I packed for her.' Whatever Mrs Arnthwaite might have been thinking, her tone gave nothing away.

Lydie bit her lip. 'Is—Mr Benedict at home?'

'He's in London with Mrs Benedict, Miss Lydie.
They're flying out to Spain tomorrow, I understand.'

'Spain?' Lydie echoed in bewilderment. 'Isn't that
rather sudden?'

'Planned as a nice surprise for Mrs Benedict,' Mrs
Arnthwaite confirmed sedately. 'And genuinely touched
she seemed too.'

'I can imagine,' Lydie returned untruthfully. In fact,
none of it made any sense at all. She took a deep breath.
'Is—is Marius about?'

'He went out a bit ago and told me not to wait up for
him tonight.' Mrs Arnthwaite's tone was faintly re-
pressive. 'I was sure you of all people would know where
he was.'

'Not necessarily.' Lydie forced a smile. 'Well—I'll let
you get on. I shall be at the gallery if anyone needs to
contact me.'

'Very good, Miss Lydie.'

Lydie drove slowly back to Thornshaugh, prey to
thoughts that pecked at her like vultures. Marius seemed
to have lost no time in starting his own healing process,
she told herself wretchedly, and there were no prizes for
guessing where he had gone or who he was with. Nadine
might not have been his first choice all those years ago,
but Lydie was certain that she would make sure she was
his second.

She wasn't used to the warehouse complex at night
and the deserted malls seemed eerie and even menacing
as she climbed the stairs to the gallery.

The first floor was a mass of shadows, and then one
detached itself from the rest and became solid reality—
a man's figure advancing silently towards her.

She wanted to scream, but the muscles in her throat
seemed suddenly paralysed.

'At last,' Marius's voice said brusquely. 'Where the hell have you been?'

'You.' Lydie almost sagged with relief. Then, aware that her heart had given an excited, treacherous leap, she straightened her shoulders and lifted her chin, glaring at him. 'What do you think you're doing, lurking in doorways like some ghastly pervert?'

'Don't overreact, Lydie.' His tone was sardonic. 'You must have been expecting me.'

'On the contrary,' she snapped back. 'I presumed you'd be obeying the dictates of your busy social life.' The image of Nadine Winton hovered painfully on the edge of her mind.

'That comes later,' he said. 'Right now we need to talk.'

She hung back. 'We've already said all that's necessary.'

'We haven't even begun,' he contradicted her flatly. He took the bunch of keys from her indignant hand, unlocked the gallery door, pushed it open and flicked the light switch. He gave her a level look. 'Will you walk in of your own accord, or shall I carry you?'

For a long moment their glances clashed, each measuring the strength of the other's will, before Lydie decided that discretion was the better part of valour.

Head high, she stalked ahead of him to the studio— no mean feat when her legs were trembling under her.

She turned, feeling like an animal at bay with the hunter closing in, and found him standing in the doorway, looking around with critical appraisal, his eyes travelling from the living area, with its elderly, comfortable furniture, to Nell's workspace, with its easel and neatly stacked canvases, and on to the big, curtained alcove and the wide bed under its patchwork quilt.

'So this is the sanctuary,' he remarked, half to himself.

She said curtly, 'Yes.' And because she needed something to occupy her and disguise the shakes she added, 'Do you want some coffee?'

His brows lifted mockingly. 'I'm glad you've decided to be civilised.'

'Don't count on it.' She filled the kettle and switched it on.

'Believe me, I count on nothing,' Marius returned equably. He took the armchair, stretching long, denim-clad legs out in front of him.

His presence made the studio seem suddenly smaller, even cramped. To cross from one side to the other would involve stepping over him, so Lydie decided to remain safely in the vicinity of the stove, busying herself with coffee-jar and beakers.

'Where's your partner?' he enquired after a moment.

'Away,' Lydie said shortly. 'Doing some heavy-duty thinking.'

'I imagine she needs to,' he said with faint grimness. 'And what about you?'

'I've already made a few decisions. When she returns I'm going to talk to her about selling the gallery.' She hesitated. 'It's not the ideal time, probably, but at least I should be able to repay Austin's loan, and Nell and I won't be tied to Thornshaugh.'

'Which is naturally important,' he agreed with that silky note in his voice that she so much detested.

'It is to me.' She poured boiling water onto the granules and stirred them. 'And may be to her.'

'So where were you this evening?' He took the proffered beaker with a brief word of thanks.

'I went to Greystones.' There was no point in prevaricating, she thought wearily. If she didn't tell him, Mrs Arnthwaite would.

'Then we must have passed each other on the road.' There was an odd note in his voice, a sudden tension in the air, tingling along Lydie's senses. 'Why did you go there?'

She looked down at the stained and waxed floorboards. There was constraint in her tone. 'I—thought my mother might need me.'

'Of course.' A definite edge this time. 'Only the bird had flown. In fact, both birds.'

'And to Spain, I understand.' She tried to speak lightly. 'Rather unexpected.'

He shrugged. 'Austin wants to look at some properties out there.' His mouth quirked slightly. 'He intends to take his retirement very seriously. He wants a warm climate and golf on his doorstep every day.'

'I see.' She stared down at her coffee, her hands clasped tightly round the beaker. 'And—my mother?'

'She'll have the local country club, tennis, bridge, the usual sangria set, no doubt.' He paused. 'And less opportunity to meddle.' He looked at her with a slight frown. 'Even with your unswerving loyalty to her, Lydie, you must see that things couldn't go on as they were. That there had to be some kind of showdown.'

'But not the kind I was expecting.' Lydie bent her head. 'I was so frightened for her. I—I didn't see how Austin could possibly understand, let alone condone what she'd done.'

'He loves her,' Marius said quietly. 'For better or worse. Through hell and high water.'

His mouth twisted slightly. 'But he also appreciates that my feelings towards her and past events are very different. And that even surface harmony between us is best maintained at a distance.'

She said quietly, 'She loves him too, Marius. I'm sure of it.' She hesitated. 'Not in the way, perhaps, that either of us would wish—' her voice faltered a little '—but as much as she's capable of.'

After another pause she asked, 'Did she explain—everything?'

'I think so. She certainly exonerated you completely, if that's what you're trying to ask.' He looked at her thoughtfully. 'Why didn't you tell me the truth when I first accused you, Lydie? Was it to protect her?'

She moved restively. 'Partly, I suppose. I knew something was terribly wrong. And also—I didn't think you'd believe me. After all, a simple denial wouldn't have meant a thing against all that evidence.'

She traced the pattern on her coffee-mug with a fingertip, before adding carefully, 'Besides, you'd had five years to convince yourself that I was guilty. You can't undo that kind of mischief in a few minutes.'

'It wasn't just one-sided, Lydie,' he said quietly.

'No.' She lifted her chin. 'I'd had to live with the idea that you'd been unfaithful. That you'd said and done all the same things to some stranger—and that she'd had your baby—'

She stopped abruptly, afraid that she'd let him see too much. 'But it's water under the bridge, isn't it?' she went on hurriedly. 'We—we can't wipe out the past. Only be sure we won't make the same mistakes again.'

'I intend to be quite certain of that.' Marius paused. 'You didn't help your cause by dropping a cheque made out to Darrell Corbin in front of me.'

That evening in the restaurant, she thought, when we seemed so close and then everything suddenly changed.

She forced a smile. 'We seem fated to misunderstand each other.' To hurt and be hurt, she added silently and painfully.

'I don't think fate had much to do with it.' His voice was dry. 'What are you going to do, Lydie, once the gallery is sold?'

She put her empty beaker in the sink and stood looking down at it. 'That's hardly your concern.'

'But I'm asking just the same,' he said levelly. 'I don't plan to spend the next five years wondering about you.'

'Or even five minutes, I hope.' There was an edge to her voice. 'Marius, I think you'd better go. I don't know why you came here...'

'Don't you? Then I'd better enlighten you. I came to you for the same reason I hoped you went to Greystones tonight. Because I couldn't stay away.'

'No.' Her hands were gripping the edge of the sink so tightly that her knuckles had turned white. 'You can't say that. You mustn't...'

'I'll say what I want.' His voice was soft, with an undertone of steel. 'That's been the problem all along— too many silences. Both of us afraid to speak—to question—in case the answers destroyed us.

'Well, those silences cost me five years in a hell of loneliness and bitterness, and I'm damned if I'll let that happen again.'

'I'd like you to go...'

'Where?' he demanded harshly. She hadn't heard him move but he was suddenly there, standing right behind her, his hands gripping her shoulders. 'Back to the wilderness of life without you? No chance.'

'You came back for revenge.' She tried to free herself to no avail. 'You told me so yourself...'

'And perhaps I even believed it—until I walked in here and saw you dancing towards me in that white and gold dress, like a lily swaying in the wind.' He laughed shakily. 'God, I was totally poleaxed. I told myself it was just the first shock of seeing you again—that it couldn't possibly be anything else—anything deeper.'

He drew a deep breath and she realised that he was trembling. 'Not until you were standing in front of all those people, about to become engaged to another man, did I realise . . .

'I tried to tell myself that he was welcome to you— that I was thankful to have any decision about you taken out of my hands. And all the time I could hear myself calling out to you as if I was drowning. Begging you to turn away from him and back to me. Just as I'm begging you now.

'Because nothing's made any difference—not the lies, the anger or the wasted years. Because I still love you— still need you as I need air to breathe. And I always will.'

His hands were gentle but inexorable as he turned her to face him. 'So, no matter where you go, or what you do, I'll follow you, Lydie, my love—my dearest love— until I make you admit that it's the same for you. That without each other there'll be nothing but emptiness and regret.'

'We can't,' she said in a half-whisper, hardly daring to believe—to hope. 'Too much has happened . . .'

'But only one thing that matters, Madonna Lily,' he said softly. 'That you and I have found each other again.'

He bent his head and kissed her mouth with yearning and an aching tenderness.

'Say it, Lydie,' he whispered against her lips. 'Tell me you love me. Don't let the lies and the pain destroy us when we've been given this second chance.'

She said with a little sob, 'I tried so hard to stop loving you. Through all those lonely years, and even this past week. But I never could. Oh, Marius . . .'

He swung her off her feet into his arms, his face alight with all the emotions she'd thought she would never see again. And she smiled back at him, her heart and soul in her eyes, as he carried her across the studio to the shadowed alcove and the waiting bed.

He placed her on the coverlet with exquisite care and sank down beside her, his mouth warm and seeking, his hands deft on the fastenings of her sleeveless shirt and jeans. She helped him in his task, her body pliant and sensuous as he undressed her between kisses before swiftly stripping off his own clothing.

They came together in a fierce, sweet intensity, with only the fever of their breathing to break the silence. The silence of intimacy instead of isolation.

Nothing existed in the world but the force of his possession pulsating inside her, carrying her away on a glorious crescendo of sensation. And as she reached the sublime peak Lydie cried out in rapture and release, and heard his voice echo hers.

A long time later he murmured, his head pillowed on her breasts, 'Now you'll have to marry me.'

'Is that a fact?' There was a tremor of laughter in her voice as she tenderly stroked the dark, sweat-dampened hair back from his forehead. 'Are you sure you don't prefer Nadine Winton?' She was, she realised, only half-joking. It was the final reassurance she needed.

'She was a convenient smokescreen,' Marius admitted unforgivably. 'But Nadine is still in love with her ex-husband, who's been making noises about a reconciliation. She asked me to meet her for a drink the other day and poured out the whole story.'

'Will she go back to him?'

He shrugged. 'She wants to, but she's afraid of being hurt all over again. She's altogether more vulnerable than she appears.'

'She's not the only one.' Lydie sighed. 'There's Neil and Jon—and Darrell Corbin too. What on earth's going to happen to them?'

'They have to solve their own problems,' Marius told her firmly. 'All that need concern us is our future together.'

He reached for his discarded shirt and took her engagement ring from its breast pocket. 'Give me your hand, Madonna Lily.'

He slid the ring onto her finger and kissed it reverently. 'From this day forward, darling.' There was an infinity of tenderness in his voice. 'Till death us do part.'

Lydie's eyes were luminous as she laced her arms round his neck and drew him down to her.

'Welcome home, my love,' she whispered, and kissed him.

Let's Celebrate!

LOVE & LAUGHTER™

invites you to
the party of the season!

Grab your popcorn and be prepared to laugh as we celebrate with **LOVE & LAUGHTER**.

Harlequin's newest series is going Hollywood!

Let us make you laugh with three months of terrific books, authors and romance, plus a chance to win a FREE 15-copy video collection of the best romantic comedies ever made.

For more details look in the back pages of any Love & Laughter title, from July to September, at your favorite retail outlet.

Don't forget the popcorn!

Available wherever
Harlequin books are sold.

 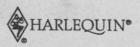 **HARLEQUIN®**

Look us up on-line at: http://www.romance.net

LLCELEB

Harlequin Women Know Romance When They See It.

And they'll see it on **ROMANCE CLASSICS**, the new 24-hour TV channel devoted to romantic movies and original programs like the special **Harlequin** Showcase of Authors & Stories.

The **Harlequin** Showcase of Authors & Stories introduces you to many of your favorite romance authors in a program developed exclusively for Harlequin readers.

Watch for the **Harlequin** Showcase of **Authors & Stories** series beginning in the summer of 1997.

ROMANCE CLASSICS

If you're not receiving ROMANCE CLASSICS, call your local cable operator or satellite provider and ask for it today!

Escape to the network of your dreams.

HARLEQUIN PRESENTS®

Indulge yourself in our spectacular
selection of top authors:

Sandra Marton
Romantic Times gold medal winner
August 1997—THE SECOND MRS ADAMS #1899

Helen Bianchin
"...tantalizing sexual tension."
—*Romantic Times*
September 1997—AN IDEAL MARRIAGE? #1905

Anne Mather
New York Times bestselling author,
with over 60 million books in print
October 1997—SHATTERED ILLUSIONS #1911

Available wherever Harlequin books are sold.